Snapshots of the Apocalypse and Other Stories

Katy Wimhurst

First published January 2022 by Fly on the Wall Press
Published in the UK by Fly on the Wall Press
56 High Lea Rd
New Mills
Derbyshire
SK22 3DP

www.flyonthewallpress.co.uk

Fly on the Wall Press is committed to the sustainable printing and shipping of their books.

Supported using public funding by
ARTS COUNCIL ENGLAND
LOTTERY FUNDED

For Lucy, Millie and Hannah.

Contents

Snapshots of the Apocalypse

Min despised the Tate Art and Refuge Centre. It contained little art and more refuse than refuge. She'd been approached by pimps in the café there, had witnessed fist-fights over chocolate, and had once seen an artwork used as a frisbee. But today, staring at the empty food cupboard in her squat, she knew she'd have to go there if she wanted to eat.

"Shit," she muttered, slamming the cupboard door.

Cursing the guy who'd yet again failed to deliver the bootleg goods, Min grabbed her bag and slung on her black PVC cape and beret. She then padlocked her squat's front door and marched down the long staircase.

On the ground floor, the sign on the wall read, THE ROYAL COL-LEGE OF URGEONS. If anyone asked 'what she did' these days, she said she was an 'urgeon'. A reasonable word, she thought, for how she kept urging herself on despite the relentless crap around – and indeed within – her. Fortunately, few asked her 'profession' these days. Had it really taken an apocalyptic world to end small talk?

The former Reception area was dusted with cobwebs, its blue carpet muddy with footprints. Min still recalled her first visit to this place years ago as a medical student, but she tried not to think of the past. That was a different era, before the floods and chaos, and she'd never finished her studies, anyway. It'd been how she'd known about this place though, and why she'd come here to hide when her flat near Tottenham Court Road had burnt down in a riot.

Outside, as ever, it was raining but thankfully it was the Cameron kind – light, unobtrusive drizzle. There were a dozen official sorts of rain, all named after previous Prime Ministers. Min's favourite was Blair, in which swirling eddies made the rain spin; she didn't mind Rashford – a refreshing spring downpour; she disliked Thatcher – hard, unforgiving; the worst was Johnson – deceptively lightweight but soaked you through-and-through.

Min hurried across the deserted Lincoln's Inn Fields. A decaying, six-storey building had cracks in its walls colonised by moss, like furry veins. She turned right, down a passageway in which was a dead oak. Two parrots perched on a branch made her eyes widen in surprise. They were kingfisher blue, defying the grey day. *How Damien would have loved them!* Remembering him, Min felt as if she was falling, but she steadied herself and continued on.

She walked down Chancery Lane, her boots splashing through puddles. Her shoulders tensed as a male voice called out from the other side of the road; keeping her gaze ahead, she picked up her pace. It wasn't safe here, but notwithstanding a mugging last year, and despite being alone, she was wily enough to have survived — so far. A phrase from somewhere popped into her head: mere survival is insufficient. *What bullshit,* she thought. Mere survival was all there was; hope belonged to another era.

When she got to the Embankment, she was relieved to find more people. London often seemed like a mausoleum these days, many having fled the city, many having died. At the Millennium Bridge, she frowned up at the building once known as Tate Modern, now the Tate Art and Refuge Centre or TARC. Its tower poked into the sky, like a one-fingered gesture at a mean cosmos.

Tired after the long walk on an empty stomach, she entered TARC and in the foyer took off her beret and shook herself to get rid of raindrops on her cape. At the turnstile, an armed guard scanned her with a weapon detector, then nodded for her to carry on. At Reception, a woman scowled at Min, but stamped her ration book and gave her a free café token. Min veered right, up one side of the Turbine Hall, avoiding the refugees and their beds in its centre.

The café was on the first floor. Handing over her token, she was given a tray containing: chicken soup, a bread roll, a chunk of cheddar cheese, an apple and tea. As she searched for a free table, she noticed a fair-haired man with a pony-tail at the edge of the room. She'd seen him in the café a couple of times before. He stood out not only because he wore a neat dark suit, but because unlike most solitary men here, he didn't try to catch her eye.

She sat at an empty, scuffed wooden table without taking off her cape – the place wasn't heated. She began to wolf down the food; the soup and bread were good. By the time she started on the apple, her energy had improved.

She was halfway through her tea when the pony-tailed man approached. "May I sit?" he asked politely, indicating the chair opposite hers.

She normally told men to piss off, but his clean-shaven face made her curious enough to take a second look: a short, handsome man with bags under his eyes. "If you must."

He sat, putting his mug of coffee on the table. He was quiet for a few minutes, just sipping his drink. Min had expected him to talk and both his silence and presence set her a little on edge.

He looked at her inquisitively. "I've noticed you here before."

"Bully for you." She took a gulp of tea.

"I thought you'd be the 'bully for you' sort."

"Bully for you. Again."

He laughed, the first genuine laugh she'd heard in ages. A stray strand of blonde hair flopped over his face and he tucked it behind his ear. "Sorry. It's just you seem different."

"Everyone's different."

"No. Everyone in this café's pretty similar. They either live as refugees downstairs, scared of what's happening, or they come in groups from outside and hang out for hours. But you, a woman alone, waltz in with that outlandish black cape, eat, then disappear."

She met the gaze of his grey-blue eyes, wondering what he wanted. "And your point is?"

"You seem fearless… or reckless."

She raised an eyebrow. "You seem full of bullshit."

He rubbed at his neck. "Would… you let me show you something?"

"If you're looking for sex, the answer's no," she snapped.

He held up his palms in a gesture of appeasement. "Sorry, I didn't mean that. Really. I'd like to show you some art."

"Oh?" She frowned. "Aren't the galleries all closed?"

"Yes, but I'm a doctor here. Well, the only doctor at present, which means I get the keys to the kingdom." He put a hand in his jacket pocket and jangled keys there.

She studied him, pondering if it were wise to trust him.

"Don't worry," he said. "I'd never make a pass at anyone with such a silly cape."

She barked a quick laugh and then wondered what age he was. As he'd completed his medical training, he must be older than her. "What's your name?"

"Max."

"Well, I'm Min."

"Really?"

"Really."

Despite her normal wariness, she was warming to this unusual man. She gulped down the rest of her tea, and then let him lead her upstairs to the second floor, where he unlocked a door of what looked like a gallery and went in. She felt a moment of fear – was it wise to follow him? Curiosity got the better of her. She took only a few steps inside, though, staying close to the entrance. A dehumidifier was humming and, when Max switched on the light, she saw large framed photographs all over the walls. Her skin tingled. *Oh, god.*

"This exhibition was *Snapshots of the Apocalypse, 2058,* by Lucy Yorke-Hirst," he said. "Do you know her work?"

"No."

Min walked slowly round the room, taking in the photographs. A skeletal man dressed in a black bin-liner stared up at the boarded-up Harrods store. A girl sat hunched in a rowing boat outside a flooded Brixton Tube, her face pale as a bone. A tower of piled-up tyres in Trafalgar Square had *Monument to Bugger-All* written on it in blue paint. A woman in a black PVC cape and beret sheltered from rain under an archway, cuddling a boy with a black PVC coat and cap.

Min felt light-headed, as if spinning. She stepped back, her eyes narrowing. "Why the fuck did you bring me here?"

"Sorry. I—"

She took a deep breath and forced herself to face Max. "You knew that was me?"

"Yes."

"You thought a trip down memory cul-de-sac would be nice?"

"I thought you might tell me about the boy." He spoke gently.

A stab of anger. "Why would I tell a stranger?"

"Because you come here alone, so I assume you lost him. I... I lost my daughter, too."

Not an answer she'd expected. As she met his candid gaze, sadness swelled inside her and she had to will the pain back. "How did you lose her?"

A muscle twitched in his neck. "A flash flood in 2056. Karina was swept away, her body never found."

"Christ!" Min pressed a hand to her chest. "I'm sorry."

"What about your boy?" he asked.

She moved close to the photograph and touched Damien's face with her fingers, feeling grief welling up. "He died in the malaria epidemic of 2057."

Max approached and placed a hand lightly on her shoulder. "I'm so sorry."

"Damien was my baby," she spluttered, and the sobs came. She let Max hold her as tears burned her cheeks. When was the last time she had been comforted like this? She could scarcely remember.

After a few minutes, when her tears stopped, she stepped back from him, becoming conscious of a slight awkwardness developing. His face was handsome but, more importantly, compassionate.

"Do you have family left in London?" he asked.

"No."

"Why do you stay here then? A single woman could easily get a Refugee Passage up North."

"London's my home. My memories of Damien are here." She drew her cape around her more tightly. "And anyway, I can look after myself."

"There are selfish people and horrible diseases here."

"Aren't there those up North, too?"

"Believe me as a medic: it's not half so bad up North and there are even parts where you can have a semi-normal life."

She let out a sigh. "I'm not sure I care anymore."

"You know, every day in my job as a doctor here, I see how life's been reduced to subsistence, suffering. Life's hard — relentlessly hard." He paused, gazing at her. "And yet, even when things are utterly shit, I still find moments of strange magic."

Min remembered the iridescent birds and looked into Max's eyes. "Perhaps I do too," she murmured.

A digi-pager beeped in his pocket. He took it out and stared at it. "Damn. I have to go."

"Pity."

"Indeed."

He led her out to the corridor, locked the door, and pointed to the right. "I'm off that way; you're not allowed there I'm afraid. But if you need anything in the future, come to TARC. Ask at Reception for Dr Max Milliband. I'll help you any way I can."

"Thank you. That's kind." She turned away quickly so he couldn't see her eyes moisten again and set off towards the stairs.

"Goodbye, Min," he called out.

"Goodbye, Max." She glanced back and waved, feeling her heart tug towards this decent stranger.

She had gone down a couple of flights of stairs to the ground floor when she heard quick footsteps behind her. She turned abruptly and Max was there, holding out a box in his right hand. "For you, my brave caped Londoner," he said. "Just in case."

She looked at the gift: antibiotics. "Thanks, you old Romantic." She smiled at him and put the drugs in her bag.

With his left hand he held out a folded piece of paper. "And here's the form to apply for refugee status up North. As I'm one of the few who can sign and approve these, you'd be a shoe-in. I promise."

"But—"

"Take it. Please fill it in. Would Damian really have wanted you to stay here?"

She hesitated, having never thought about it like that before. Damian was a caring boy who used to save scraps of food for the birds even when Min and he had little. He'd have hated that her life was mere survival; he'd have wanted her safe. Before she could choke up with tears again, she took the form, thanked Max, placed it in her bag, turned on her heels, and headed off towards the Exit.

Outside, Thatcher rain was falling, and Min clutched onto her bag as if it were a life-buoy.

In the Shadow of The Egg

We lived on the outskirts of town, so looking east from the garden on a sunny day like this we could see The Egg. Dad and I came out of the poly-tunnel, where we were sowing salad leaves, and we stopped to stare. "Maybe they breed cyborg dragons there," I said as a joke.

"Don't talk rubbish." The grim lines of Dad's mouth corners always made it seem like he was disapproving of something.

I wished again I could leave home.

What was made or done at The Egg? No one knew. The many rumours – that biotech was being produced or genetically-modified animals were being bred – were all dismissed by the government who held locals only need know one thing: it was a research centre.

I heard coughing and twisted my head towards the house. Mum was at the kitchen window, gripped by a fit.

"Shut the window," I called out.

"Don't give her ideas. It's not the smoke," said Dad.

"For Christ sake. Why do you believe that Simon Darkhorse?"

"Dr Darkhorse writes common sense," said Dad.

"Common sense, my arse," I said. *Forget any mumbo-jumbo going around,* the town council leader and former psychiatrist had written in his column in *The Gazette. Scientific tests have refuted that these coughs and migraines are in any way linked to the smoke. The increase in illness is most likely psychosomatic.*

Dad flicked a hand to dismiss me and headed towards his greenhouse; we grew our own fruit and vegetables as they were scarce and pricey.

I stood frowning at The Egg: built about a year ago and laminated in mirror glass, the oval building loomed around 90m high and 70m wide over the plain, like some giant, fairy-tale, silver egg planted in the ground – hence its nickname; and like a fairy tale, it held secrets. It winked in the sun and a thin stream of smoke billowed from the 100m tower beside it, ash from a cosmic cigarette.

A shiver crept down my spine so I headed inside to change; as all my chores were done I planned to meet Aylia. Mum was in the kitchen, leaning on her crutches and wheezing. She was short and slender like me, her brow permanently etched with worry, and her symptoms made her seem more fragile. I fetched her a glass of water and waited until her chest eased. "Keep the windows closed," I said.

"Dad says it isn't that."

"Dad says a lot of things."

"Don't take that tone, Cass." Her eyes, grey-blue like mine but lined with crows-feet, fixed upon me. "If it's The Egg, why aren't people like Damon getting ill?"

I shrugged. It was a good question, the only one that brought me any doubts. Why were those who worked up there in good health?

"Off to see Aylia?" she asked.

"Yes."

"Don't come back so drunk again."

"Mum. I'm twenty."

Before we lived in 'the shadow of The Egg', as Aylia and I called it, she and I used to go for long rambles in the hills. Now, because the hills had – for an unknown reason – been declared off limits to local people, we met in town. I tensed on seeing two militia police coming towards me on Guin Street and slid my hand into my inside jacket pocket, feeling for my ID card, but a woman just ahead started coughing and the two stepped off the pavement to give her a wide berth, hardly clocking me.

I found Aylia on the bench outside the library reading a book. Her hair, tugged into an unruly pony-tail, had been dyed with that faintly phosphorescent indigo colour, and it matched the tight indigo tee-shirt she wore over jeans. She looked up and smiled in her lopsided way; her topaz eyes sparkled, as did the silver ring in her nose. In this stagnant pond of a town, she was an alluring dragonfly. "Hey, girlfriend," she said.

"Good hair," I said.

She put a slender hand to her head. "You should try this colour. It would suit you."

"You know I can't." These days I wore my dark hair in a long bob with a fringe, which made looking respectable on weekdays easier. "Good book?"

"Excellent for nerds like me." She stuffed it in her rucksack and stood. She had an athletic frame and was taller than me. "Let's go in."

Two years ago Aylia had won a scholarship to a good university in the south. I'd been gutted, having applied unsuccessfully; and while I'd worried that her going away would put more than physical distance between us, it had actually brought us closer. "You're my bestie, the only person I can really speak to in this shithole," she would say when home.

The town's library was among its best assets: a beautiful old gothic building with elaborate turrets and an entry alcove lined with sculptured scenes of the Last Judgement – 'doom in stone' as Aylia and I called it. After perusing the shelves inside for a while, Aylia checked out a couple of crime thrillers for her mum, and I checked out a book on growing summer fruits, and two Margaret Atwood novels – written 40 years back, in the early 2000s, they were still prescient.

Outside, Alyia asked, "Is the fruit book for Mr Misery Gutes?" Her eyes glinted with mischief.

It was her name for my dad, our surname being Gutes. "Yup."

"How's your mum, by the way?"

"Still got the bad cough."

"Keep the windows closed and get an air purifier."

"Dad still refuses to accept it's because of The Egg."

"Does he always have to be a Grade A moron?"

"He's just fitting in, in this town."

"The offer is still there, Cass. The spare sofa bed in my bedroom would do you for the first month or so and there's always waitressing and shop work to be found."

"You know I can't." It was nice to fantasise about escaping, but realistically it wasn't on the cards. Dad had tried to find more than part-time work, but there were so few jobs around. "My work isn't so bad."

"You're destined for better things than Turncoat Ballistics."

I laughed. "It's Waincoate Logistics." The job was a bit dull and administrative, but at least meant I could get away from Mum and Dad during the day; my boss was decent too and sent me off on training courses. "Anyway, wherever you go, it's the same shit, isn't it, The Shortages still The Shortages, the government still the government." Mum had told me about growing up in the time before The Shortages, when the shop

17

shelves were full and everyone had cars, computers and smart phones; she and Dad had actually met through this online thing called *Instagrab* or *Instagram*.

Aylia glanced around to check no one was in earshot, then spoke quietly. "But you wouldn't feel so alone. *Resist* is stronger in the city."

I shrugged.

"Living here has made you defeatist. No one can fight those bastards alone, but *Resist* is growing — why not be part of that too? I told you ten thousand of us gathered for a street protest last month?" she said.

"Yes." At the time I'd heard nothing in the media here. I didn't want to talk about it, though, as it seemed a world away and what difference would it make anyway? "Come on. I need a beer."

Aylia and I wandered all the way up Orwell Street, past the fence plastered with graffiti — *Less Work, More Wine; Is This Our Best (De)Fence?* — and along to the Bleeding Keel Bar. They played indie tunes from the 2030s there, which made us happy and nostalgic; Aylia and I'd hit our early teens in the middle of that decade.

"All packed to go back?" I asked when we'd bought beers and settled into our seats.

"I'll pack tomorrow. Getting the 8am on Monday. Can't wait. I'll miss you, though, Cass."

"We'll write."

"You'd bloody better, girlfriend."

Some hot bloke with impressive pectorals and those Colenses that created geometric patterns in irises came over and asked if he could buy us drinks, but we said no. Watching him walk away, Aylia muttered to me, "If it were anything other than our last night together, I'd do him."

"Jesus, A. Don't you ever stop?" She drifted like a petal in the breeze from one boyfriend to another, so much so that I lost track.

"Speaking of blokes, have you seen Damon?" she asked.

"I'm back in my holding pattern of neglecting the poor guy."

"Not sure why he doesn't tell you to do one."

"A! He's not my boyfriend."

"Treating him like shit would be more understandable if he was."

She had a point. Whenever Aylia went back to university, I'd feel lonely again and go back to hanging out with Damon, who lived on the next road.

It was a dull road of semi-detached houses like mine. When I rang his doorbell after a few weeks' absence, he opened the door and asked tersely, "Your girlfriend left you for the city again?" Damon was pale and scrawny with an expression too serious for a lad of nineteen. His acne hadn't flared up for a while so his skin looked better under the floppy brown fringe that fell over his eyes.

"You want to do something tonight?" I asked.

"Sorry, Cass. Got something else planned."

"Bullshit, you have." He only ever wore his old *Paranoid Android* tee-shirt when staying in. "Look, I know I've been a crap friend, but here's my liquid apology." I opened my bag to show two bottles of wine.

"Oh, alright, come on up."

I followed his gawky form up the stairs and into his bedroom.

I told myself that we both got something out of this: me, someone to share my loneliness with, and him, free booze and someone who could match his skill at card and computer games. But in truth I took him, and the crush he'd had on me for years, for granted. Occasionally when drunk I'd quiz him about The Egg. "What do you do up there?"

"For Christ sake! Stop asking that."

"Okay, okay." No one working there was allowed to say anything.

I plonked myself on his single bed and put my palm out. "Come on then. Let's play."

He laid down next to me with the *Zikka* tablophone he'd got given with his job, a sleek 5x7 inch device few could afford, and we took it in turns to play our favourite game, Dragon Crush.

"Kill that Elixir Dragon with your missile," he exclaimed, pointing to the screen.

"I'm saving my missile for any Zone Dragons."

"You always do that wrong."

I sang: "But more, much more than this, I killed it myyyyy waaaaay."

Damon laughed and then joined in as I sung it again.

On Sunday, when I was nursing a hangover, Dad told me at break-

19

fast about Simon Darkhorse's new theory of the origin of the coughing. "People started going down with it around the time the Dutch came."

"Jesus. He really wrote that?" The Dutch were climate-change refugees from across the channel and a number were housed in this town.

"Well, it's common sense if you think about it."

"It's bullshit. The first Dutch arrived over a year before The Egg was even built."

"Yes, but the dormitories in that old school weren't full of them until nine months back."

"Simon Darkhorse is just stoking prejudice to shift blame. Don't fall for it, you idiot."

His mouth tightened. "Dr Darkhorse knows what he's talking about. More than can be said for you."

"He's a former psychiatrist. What the hell does he know about pollution or whatever it is in the air?"

"He's done more in life than you ever will."

I glared before storming out of the room, leaving my toast half eaten. He knew full well the reason I hadn't gone off to go university was that they depended on my wage; with her arthritis Mum couldn't work. Had I won a scholarship like Aylia, I could have put some of that money their way, but without it, study was impossible.

The next weekend, after Damon and I had necked a bottle of vodka, I asked, "Sure they don't give you some antidote up at The Egg?"

"Shut up about that, will you?" His speech was slurry with drunkenness, but he was looking at me with that besotted puppy face.

Maybe that is why I said: "Tell me the truth and I'll snog you."

"You... mean it?"

"Why not?" I didn't fancy him, but once wouldn't hurt.

His brow curdled to a frown.

I leaned my face close to his. "Don't you want a kiss?"

His pupils dilated, meaning he was tempted. "Promise you won't say anything?"

"Promise," I whispered in his ear.

"I mean it. Tell anyone – even Aylia – and I might get in deep shit. I had to sign some form saying I'd say nothing on pain of losing my job."

"Trust me."

He spoke quietly. "There seem to be some kind of air purifiers going 24/7, though no-one is entirely sure what they are. We also have to drink a small packet of this white powder in water every day. They say it's a perk of the job, just vitamins and minerals, but my health has never been better. Hardly get any acne outbursts or colds or even hangovers now."

"The powder is medicine?"

"It's something." He went in for the kiss, slipping in an unwelcome tongue. If I hadn't been pissed and grateful, I'd have pushed him off.

After work on Monday, I attended a local meeting in the community hall on Easter Street. *Dutch Go Home* was newly graffitied on its fence. It was too late to get a seat so I edged down the heaving room and stood to one side. I waved hellos to several familiar faces.

The panel of four at the front included Simon Darkhorse. The short introductory speeches each gave drew mixed reception – cheers and boos – from the audience. Simon Darkhorse got the most applause; god knows why for a government stooge adept at talking bollocks. I felt for the Dutch woman called Sara who ran a refugee advice service in town and had to make her voice heard over heckling. "If the health problems came from us Dutch, why aren't other towns afflicted in the same way?"

"Are we sure information isn't being suppressed?" called a sour-faced, balding man in the audience.

"What about the smoke?' barked someone.

A few cries of 'nonsense' rippled through the audience. Simon Darkhorse's gaze scoured the hall like that TrackCam in town, scanning faces. "Who said that? Want to stand up and speak properly?"

No one put their hand up. Should I say something? Millie Barber, who'd been a year above me at school, stood up. She fiddled with her bead necklace. "It wasn't me who spoke just now, but... can we rule out the smoke completely? Is the science robust enough?"

My heart began to thump, as if prompting me, and I found myself raising my hand. "I... I agree with the last speaker. Don't we need more data before we rule out the smoke?" Millie nodded an acknowledgement my way.

"This is alarmism and mumbo jumbo." Simon Darkhorse's hand karate chopped the air. "The science says the smoke isn't a problem."

I was momentarily tempted to say I'd heard something about air purifiers and powdered medicine, but all eyes, many unfriendly, were on me, and surely my words could be traced back to Damon.

"Well?" Simon Darkhorse folded his arms.

I shook my head and felt a flush of relief as all those eyes swivelled away.

A tense discussion ensued in the hall, which achieved little more than a thin whitewash of reality. When I left later, several people threw scowls my way, and on the way home, militia police appeared twice to check my ID card, once on Borne Road, once on Violet Street. I'd never been stopped more than a few times a week before.

At dinner on Wednesday evening, Mum said, "Did you hear Damon got fired?"

Oh, god, no. "Why?" I croaked.

"No idea. He's a good lad. Can't imagine him giving any employer problems."

"Must have had a reason for giving him the boot," said Dad curtly.

Cold crept down my back. The Egg couldn't have known about his and my conversation, could they? Damon wasn't the sort to say anything.

I slept badly that night, but it was two days before urgency propelled me to Damon's door. His eyes looked bloodshot when he opened it. "What do you want?"

"Are you okay?"

"Why would you care?"

Why was he being arsey? "Heard you lost your job. What happened?"

He glanced behind to check his mum and dad weren't within earshot, then stepped outside and drew the door partly closed. "Didn't have you down as a blabbermouth, Cass."

"What? I've said nothing."

"Don't bullshit me."

"What do you think I am? Who would I have told, anyway?"

His expression segued from irritation to perplexity. "Is that… the truth?"

"Of course."

"Shit!" He pushed the door further open and grabbed a jacket off a rail, then closed it completely. "Let's walk."

In St John's Road, Damon kept glancing behind, as if checking no one was following. Who would be, I wondered, my gut tightening with tension. We hurried to the old church on the corner. The bench in the churchyard was somewhere he and I had hung out as kids. Gauzy sunlight crept through gaps in the grey marble sky and clusters of daffodils spilled from some graves.

When we'd sat down, I said, "Tell me."

Scratching at his neck, he talked quietly. "My manager knew I'd said something to someone about the powder. He let it slip by accident just before he fired me. He also told me to keep my mouth shut about The Egg, said they'd deny everything and make life very difficult if I went public. Sure you said nothing to anyone? Not even in a letter to Aylia?"

"Of course not." I thought for a minute, my pulse racing. "You don't think they've bugged your bedroom?"

"Doesn't make sense. How could they bug all employees' rooms or houses without someone noticing something?"

I remembered an article I'd read years ago about surveillance during the internet years. "Does the tablophone have a mike?"

He winced as his fists clenched shut. "Crap! That never occurred to me. I've had to give the thing back, but yes, they were probably listening in on it."

"Shit," I said. "What will you do about work?"

"Got a job lined up packing at the Cartright warehouse. Have to do that until something better comes up." He heaved a sigh.

We sat in silence, me scanning the rows of gravestones and feeling the prickle of both guilt and worry. Was he on a Watch List now? Was I? A jolt of anger went through me. How dare they treat Damon like this! I wanted to do something, but what? Was there a branch of *Resist* here? "Bloody Egg, bloody government," I said.

"And no more Zombie Crush."

"That's the worst part," I said wryly.

"God, yes."

I think he was serious.

Back at Damon's house, I said, "I'd better not come round yours this Saturday." I was hoping he'd tell me not to be daft, but he avoided my eye, saying, "Sensible plan."

That Saturday night, with no Damon or Aylia, I asked Millie Barber if she wanted to go for a drink. Both in jeans and tee-shirts, we sat in the The Anchor, laughing about the past – teachers we'd disliked and blokes we'd fancied at school. After a few beers, I blurted out, "Know anything about *Resist* here?"

"Shush," she cautioned, glancing around nervously. "Don't your parents depend on your income?"

She meant what would happen if I ended up in jail. "So you do know something?"

Her eyes studied me. "Drop it, Cass."

After more beers, I asked again, but she cut me dead. Maybe, even if she was involved, me asking so openly had flagged me as a bad recruit.

Walking home alone later, I stared up at the bloated moon, thinking how much I wanted out of this town. I was stopped on Winston Road by a militia policeman with a surly face, who demanded to see my ID. "Cassandra Gutes. Is that a Dutch name?"

"No."

"Are you drunk, Miss Gutes?"

"No."

He smirked. "Well, run along home. You never know who might be out there to prey on a lone girl at night."

Was his intent to patronise or unsettle? I hurried home but didn't sleep well. In the morning, still unsure about the man's tone, an unease I couldn't shake off settled over me.

On Monday, I came home from work to find takeaway pizza on the table. We couldn't afford takeaways normally. Dad and Mum were smiling too. When had that last happened?

"I got Damon's old job at The Egg," Dad explained. "I phoned them when I heard he was fired and went for an interview today."

"Great." In truth, I had mixed feelings: guilt over Damon, but relief too as this meant my parents would no longer depend on my wage. "What kind of job is it?"

"Can't say. You know that. Now let's eat."

Dinner at home was normally a subdued affair, three people who existed in an easily shaken truce, but today we ate and chatted, them in fine spirits, me pretending all was good.

What do you call someone who inadvertently shafts her friend but ends up opening a door for herself in the process? Luckily cursed? Cursedly lucky? That was me. The next morning, I dug out old university prospectuses from two years back. On lunch break from work later, I contacted various admissions departments. No way would I get into Aylia's university, but there was a less prestigious one in the same city that told me my exam results would get me on a degree in biology. My heart raced with excitement.

I handed in my notice at work. It was four months before my degree would start, but I intended to take Aylia up on her offer of a sofa bed and to look for work in the city.

I had to work four weeks' notice so said nothing to Mum and Dad until the final one, worried they might kick off. But when I eventually confessed, Mum hugged me and Dad, settled at the Egg, nodded enthusiastically. "Study hard, Cassandra, but don't you dare get involved in that commie *Resist*."

I swivelled my gaze to the air purifier he'd bought the week before. Mum's cough had consequently improved. I had every intention of getting involved in *Resist*.

Just before leaving town, I used my final paycheque to buy Damon a gift: a second-hand gamester to play Dragon Crush on; I'd found it in *Electronic Odds and Sods*. He hugged me, saying, "I'll miss you."

On the morning of my departure, as the train pulled out of the station, I stared out at the walls glazed in graffiti either side of the tracks: *Tez Woz Here; Resist!; Fuck the Cistern*. As the train built speed, leaving The Egg behind and coming out into countryside doused in sun, I twiddled with a strand of dyed indigo hair and couldn't stop smiling.

Haunted by Paradise

It is spring – plants are covering the earth in drifts of green. But the only vegetation inside Eva's small, rented flat on the second floor of a house in Edenvale Street, Hammersmith, is a solitary daffodil in a plastic pot. She wanders around the flat, sighing. The floral wallpaper in the living room is torn and faded; the chipped, lime-green bedroom paint is like the aftermath of a bad rave party; and even sunbeams creep cautiously through the windows and then retreat, realising they have come across a place more suited to twilight.

Eva looks sullenly at an Xbox, power drill and cardboard cut-out of Homer Simpson in a corner of the living room. Relics of Adam, her ex, they clutter up the space. He'd walked out on her a fortnight ago; she'd returned from work to find a goodbye note saying that he wanted children, while she – aged thirty-seven now – seemed unable to conceive. It ended: *Will pop back for the rest of my things sometime.*

The casualness of 'pop' still makes her want to cut Homer in half. Pop – a word for going to the corner shop, not for collecting things from someone you lived with for five years. 'I'll give you pop,' she mutters. She gathers as much of his stuff as she can hold, marches it downstairs, and dumps it into next-door's skip. Three trips to the skip later, having purged the flat, Eva texts Adam: *Popped all your things in number 6's skip. Suggest you pick them up pronto.*

That'll teach him, she thinks, but her hands are trembling.

With a cup of chamomile tea, she sits down on her sofa and, to distract herself, opens a favourite book about Derek Jarman's garden at Dungeness. Look at all the amazing plants the film-maker managed to grow on a bleak pebble beach near the nuclear power station – peony, Star-of-Bethlehem, sweet pea, allium, borage, cotton lavender, acanthus. One sentence makes her heart jolt, and she says it aloud, tasting its encouragement: "I'd like anyone who reads this book to try some wildness in a corner."

A strange idea flies to her. She hurries to the nearest garden centre where she buys five bags of compost and twenty shade-loving plants. Back at the flat, she hauls the bedroom furniture down to the shared basement and then rushes upstairs again. By evening, dripping with sweat, Eva has replaced the double bed with something like a garden – tall stands of pink foxgloves, white pools of wood anemones and feathery-leafed ferns. She stretches her arms out, tips her head back, and twirls round in joy. That night she sleeps naked on a bed of soft compost, covered with a tartan rug.

Next morning, Eva phones the IT office where she works to tell them she is sick, and then starts on the living room. In a deep bed of peat, she plants five young fruit trees. Around them she puts the flowers of spring: bluebells, tulips and daffodils. Her love of clay modelling returns and she fashions twelve birds out of clay. They are no larger than finches and she paints them cobalt blue with bright yellow beaks. Over a glass of wine that evening, staring at her garden, drunk with joy, she thinks: *When was the last time I felt this good?*

Eva uses some savings to take long-term leave from work. Most days she tours the local parks with a surreptitious trowel and large bag, her heartbeat scooting in excitement, and she returns home later to plant the stolen green goods. When there is no space left in the living room and bedroom, she colonises the kitchen and bathroom. Through the permanently open windows, winds bring seeds, and poppies and dandelions soon spring up. Eva never weeds them out, hoping they've been blown there by the breath – or the farts – of angels.

Soon, the garden takes on a life of its own, which makes Eva quiver in delight. Plants grow with an unnatural speed and vigour. Flowers blossom in purples, blues, pinks, oranges and yellows. Small saplings morph swiftly into trees, the branches of which offer ripe plums, apples and cherries. Climbing lilies spread over the trees in a profusion of red. Star-shaped vines grow down from the ceilings and glow with an unearthly light. Eva's clay models come alive, turning into little birds that flit from branch to branch and sing arias so pure they make her cry. A snake with green lozenges down its back slithers into a tree, coils itself around a branch, and hangs there like some strange, tempting fruit. She stares up at it, mesmerised.

The magical transformation of the garden is mirrored by changes in Eva. The heat from the rich ecosystems makes clothes superfluous; she goes naked and no longer leaves the flat. She runs her palms over her soft, round belly, and pokes her toes into the rich, dark soil. She no longer frets about the past or future, and her world-weariness vanishes, belonging it seems to some distant era of commuting and offices. She dwells in an absorbing present, one of the brush of grasses against skin, the scent of gardenias and jasmine, the thrill of peacock butterflies landing on outstretched arms, the taste of cherries and contentment.

Time is no longer measured by clock or calendar, but by cyclical rhythms, the passage of day and night, the waxing and waning of the moon. By day, Eva tends the garden with great care, and feasts on the succulent cherries and plums and salad leaves harvested from it. By night, she stares at the sky, which has become a blue stained-glass window, framed by the dark patterns of intertwining branches. In a trance-like state, she dances in and out of the trees. She writes lines of poetry on the walls, using a finger dipped in red ink from fresh beetroot: *Holy the flowers! Holy the ferns! Holy the flesh!* She lives in a continuum of gentle ecstasy and organic sensuality, as if in some sacred sentient place. *Nothing can ruin this earthly paradise,* she thinks. *Nothing!*

One day comes a loud knock. The hall is so overgrown that she can only reach the door by crawling through a mass of undergrowth. Opening the door, she makes out a male figure. At first, she cannot see him clearly as sunlight pouring through the landing window haloes him in gold. As her eyes adjust, she recognises an old man with a long white beard – it is her landlord. But he glances down, not meeting her eye.

Oh god, I'm naked, she thinks, and grabs some leaves to cover her private parts.

"You're being evicted," the landlord says. "You have two hours to gather your things and leave the flat, or the bailiffs will remove you by force."

Eva's throat goes dry, her arms start to tremble. "But... why?"

"Look at all that!" He points to all the vegetation behind her. "What the hell have you been doing? Plus you haven't paid the rent in months and the neighbours all complained." The landlord shakes his head in disgust. "I'm a respectable man, a religious man. What you've done here isn't civilised, it isn't Godly."

So Eva is cast out of paradise into the primitive chaos that is 21st-century London. She feels torn, hopelessly adrift. Being completely broke, she has no choice but to move into a friend's tiny spare room in Peckham, which overlooks a noisy kebab shop. "From paradise to Peckham," she exclaims, and sobs for hours, curled up in bed.

Eva tries to return to her job in IT, but the yearning for paradise tugs too hard at her heart. She manages to get a job as an assistant gardener in a public park, tending flower beds, clipping hedges; that eases the ache a little. One day, at a lecture in Kew Gardens, she meets a middle-aged garden-centre manager who, over a glass of wine later, admits he owns twelve books on roses, seven on irises; her heart races. After their first date, she is thrilled to receive a postcard from him of a magnolia tree, which says: *I think I've found my soil mate*. After a whirlwind romance, most of it spent on long walks, discussing plant species, they move in together to a terraced cottage in Middlesex and grow rare species of orchids.

Not for a year can Eva venture back to Edenvale Street. Then she knocks tentatively on the door of her former downstairs neighbour.

"Oh, it's you," he says, lip curling with distaste.

She asks him what happened to her old flat.

He grins smugly. "It was sold to a property developer who's gentrifying the area. Some contractors hacked out all the plants. It took them ages as there were so many. They then fitted the flat with tasteful, minimalist décor and sold it as a bachelor pad to a corporate lawyer."

Bastards, she thinks, *bastards, bastards*.

Although Eva's garden no longer exists, she still occasionally goes back to Edenvale Street. She's heard the rumours that, if you walk down the road on warm summer evenings, you may encounter a cobalt-blue bird with a song so exquisite and sad that it sounds like a lost fragment of heaven.

The Wings of Digging

After ensuring his safety helmet is done up, Arek spreads his wings and lifts off. He flies up past the scaffolding, heart pumping, breath coming fast. He glances left. What a view! The Queen Elizabeth Olympic Park with its silver-roofed velopark, the Thames glimmering pewter in the distance. As always, he wishes he could fly whenever and wherever he wants.

He lands on a wooden platform, holds fast to a scaffolding pole, and folds his wings back behind his shoulders. Not much wind today, even up here. Inside the scaffolding, he steps along the platform towards the two workmen, one lithe, one stocky.

"Check-in," he says.

Both men's foreheads curdle into frowns. Arek's clipboard, which he takes out of his bag, reminds him of their names; he deals with a lot of workmen across the site. They talk him through what they have done so far that day, and he notes it down, asking follow-up questions to ensure all points on the Management Checklist are covered. Arek is uneasy being an Eye, doesn't get why management needs to keep such extensive tabs on workers, but it pays better than any other job he could get, certainly better than the abattoir.

Flying building to building, Arek completes sixteen check-ins across the site, then swoops down to take the worksheets to the site manager's office.

Mr Slater has blue veins on his red, bulbous nose, the colours match the Crystal Palace flag on his wall. He takes the check-in sheets, slapping them on his desk. "I got bad news for you, my son," he says. "Marc's bloody well gone and broken his arm."

Arek glances down, knowing what is coming.

"Which means your leave is well and truly cancelled."

It's hard arguing with Mr Slater. In a bad mood, he fires those who talk back. Arek is aware that his wings, tucked inconspicuously behind his back, will be changing from their normal chartreuse shimmer to the mustard colour they take on when he is disappointed.

"Wipe that look off your chops. You told me you'd got no plans. Just take the leave in a month or so. Now give us your Flying Permit and get lost." Mr Slater holds out his broad palm.

Taking off the fluorescent-green wristband, Arek hands it to Mr Slater, who shoves it straight into the safe.

Outside, in the late afternoon sun, Arek's shoulders stoop. "Shit," he mutters. The dig is the only thing he has been looking forward to for months. Arek hasn't told Mr Slater about his plans as he doesn't want his workmates knowing he is volunteering on a dig; doesn't want the barrage of comments that will ensue. Once, down the pub, he had made the mistake of telling them his real passion was for archaeology. For months they took the piss out of him, which made him so tense he bit all his nails to the quick. Some teasing was light-hearted: "Peed in an ancient pot last night then, Arek?" Some went further: "Poncy bloody Floatas thinking they're better than us."

Arek glances back at Mr Slater's office. Why not go and argue, even hand in his notice? Then, as ever when a brush with authority looms, his chest pounds. *Get real,* he tells himself. He is lucky to have this job. Nevertheless, he sends texts to a few mates asking if they know an Eye to cover at short notice. It's a long-shot and he's unsure if Mr Slater would agree, anyway.

At the bus stop, both humans and Floatas wait huddled up. One grey-haired human scowls at him; he could do without the racists today. Messages skip across the notice board: *56 to Islington Due 18.43pm; No Flying Except When Working,* followed by a black cross over a pair of wings. That icon makes Arek's toes curl. Why did two of the 'Floata Rights Now!' lot deliberately crash feet-first through an upper window of the House of Commons last year? Surely they knew it would be used as an excuse to make the laws on flying even harsher.

The bus takes Arek all the way to Holloway. He's normally philosophical, but today his heart feels soldered to the bus floor. A text comes: *Can't do next week, m8. You'll be lucky getting anyone at this short notice...* Arek alights from the bus outside Dotty's Bagels and, to console himself, goes in for a pastry. The shop smells comforting, like childhood. Back in his homeland, his parents had run a bakery which they lived above, and every day when he got home from school, they'd give him a sticky bun before he went upstairs to do homework. Now, he eats the cinnamon slice as he walks along, calling an image to his mind of writing essays while his parents served Danish pastries and doughnuts downstairs. It seems too innocent, too good a time to have existed, but remembering helps him hold a sense of who he is.

At the library round the corner, he drops in to pick up two books: *Under Another Sky: Journeys in Iron Age Britain*, and *Wings and Arrows: Floatas in Roman Britain*. It was through visiting libraries back home that Arek had first discovered he wanted to be an archaeologist. He'd flicked through a book about Minoan art and felt an adrenalin rush as he'd read a caption saying the small figure on one pot wasn't a mythical being but an early depiction of a Floata. After that, he'd read everything he could get his hands on. Knowing Floatas have an acknowledged place in ancient cultures still makes his heart quicken and the world seem full of possibility.

Further down the road, he takes the shortcut through the little urban park. *FORREN FLOATERS OUT*, says the graffiti on a wall, *WINGS AINT NATURAL*. Arek turns his face away. The footpath goes past a children's sandpit in which two young girls are playing. "Hey!" the taller cries and pelts towards him, followed by the other. She stops; her white socks wrinkle round her ankles and her piercing blue eyes stare out beneath a fringe of ginger curls. "Show us your wings," she says.

"No."

She wipes her runny nose on her sleeve. "Please!"

"Go on!" the other girl joins in.

He checks the park is empty. His pulse accelerates as he unfolds his wings, which are pale and semi-transparent and woven through with thick dark veins. They look soft and gossamer, but are muscular and dense, the shape of a Swallowtail butterfly's with a chartreuse shimmer.

"So pretty." The ginger girl's eyes light up like bulbs. "Can I touch them?"

The second girl nudges the first. "Mum says you can get sick from touching 'em."

"Your Mum's wrong," he says firmly. "That simply isn't true." He folds the wings back, and continues towards home. How foolish to risk that for two snotty girls, but at least he enjoyed seeing their excited faces.

Back home, *One Day I'll Fly Away* blasts from the radio in the communal living room. He grimaces and hurries up the stairs on which the banisters are missing. On the second floor, he unlocks the padlock to his room and goes in. The single bed is unmade, and he opens the cracked window for air. "Shit," he says. "Shit."

At his desk, he boots his old laptop and opens the Caerleon dig blog. Each evening he keeps up to speed, and he checks out a photo of a new find: half a small statue of (probably) Minerva. Normally, he finds that archaeology offers the grand historical vision that puts everything in perspective – societies come and go, empires rise and fall. But staring at the blog today, perspective fails him; all he can see is work next week. Memories unlock from last summer: working in a trench, using a paint brush and spatula to tease out from the ground what turned out to be a lead amulet; washing trays of dirty stony matter and picking out Roman pottery shards. All the others on the dig had been students or lecturers. For him, it had been a cheap holiday and more importantly a time doing what he knows is his calling.

On the windowsill is a photo of his parents. Standing on the bakery steps back home, his dad's expression is proud, and his mum, with her kindly smile, holds up a silver plate of cupcakes like an offering. The photo is from that more innocent time, before they were forced into the ghetto by the law prohibiting Floatas from owning businesses. Arek's gaze lifts to the cracked windowpane. In emails to them back home, he airbrushes out unpleasant details, lets them believe his current life in England is better than it is; he is sure they do the same with him. He wishes again that they had paid for him to be smuggled as a refugee somewhere other than England – Norway or New Zealand where Floatas have better opportunities. But how were they to know?

The sky outside is fading to dusk. The two things he loves most in life are flying and archaeology, going up in the air and under the ground, yet he is forced to spend most of his time on the flat surface of subsistence.

At dinner time, he goes downstairs. Em is serving everyone the stew and baked potatoes she has cooked, which smell good. Dinner is as ever a hectic, noisy event. The lads talk about the football results. Anya tells a story about some punter at her bar getting his 'bits' trapped in his zipper; as she cackles, her wings become more intensely pink. Arek glances at Em sitting next to him. The other guys in the house all fancy Anya, but it's Em that Arek could hang his heart on, she's lithe and resourceful with a quiet, determined intelligence. She has the loveliest wings too – dragonfly

-shaped with a faint blue-green sheen. Not that she'd be interested, men aren't her thing, nor Anya's, for that matter.

Em's fine dark hair hangs straight to her shoulders. "How was work?" she asks.

"Bit shit. My leave's cancelled. Another Eye broke his arm."

"Oh, no." She fixes him in her gaze. "Your boss does know you're meant to be going to Wales, right?"

His attention slides to his plate, but he says nothing.

"Why not tell him?" she asks.

"You know why."

"Don't be a wuss. It's worth a shot, surely?"

Should he? If Arek thinks about standing up to Mr Slater, his palms sweat. He's never been assertive; even at school he was timid, kept his mouth shut. At fourteen, when the situation was getting worse back home, he'd deliberately stopped winning the local Floata skydiving prize as that had made him a target of some human kids. They'd held him down in the toilets at school and tied loo rolls with string to his wings. He'd learned then that being unseen was better than being the centre of a scene.

"Talk to the bloke," says Em. "Promise me, Arek?"

Em is right. What's there to lose – apart from months of piss take, that is. "Okay."

"Have you signed up for night school again in September?"

"Not yet. Feels like it's taking forever to get UniCerts"

"Tell me about it."

Her pretty brown eyes look so tired tonight he wishes he could reach out and touch her as a comfort, but she might pull away, leaving him embarrassed.

"Anya told me you used to go on digs back home," she says. "Is that true?"

"One dig, yes. In Mexico when I was seventeen." By writing an essay, he'd won an award to go and join a dig among Mayan ruins for three weeks one summer. He remembers it fondly, especially as it was in the last period of relative normality before The Troubles began.

Her smile reveals dimples. "Jesus. At that age I was going to the mall with friends."

"I've never wanted to be anything but an archaeologist."

"One day. You're only twenty-two."

Arek tosses and turns in bed that night. At 6.30 am, he wakes abruptly to a text arriving from a mate: *Bloke called Jono sometimes covers leave on building sites. Has Level 8 Health & Safety clearance. Number 07765 453656.*

Good news, possibly. Arek sends Jono a text.

That morning, Arek grabs his phone every time a text arrives, but none are from Jono. He decides to talk to Mr Slater regardless and goes to the office, anxiety tugging at his gut.

"What do you want?" barks Mr Slater.

"About next week—"

"Not got time for this. Get lost." Mr Slater gestures to the door.

Arek hears Em's voice in his head: *promise me, Arek.* "I… I did have plans. Just hadn't told you."

"Too bad."

"But I may have found someone experienced to cover."

Mr Slater sighs. "Not happy about this, but you're a hard worker. Might as well fill me in. This better be good."

As he explains where he's due to go, Mr Slater looks at Arek like he's said he's going to leap over the moon on a donkey. A mean amusement then flickers in the man's eyes, as if he can't wait to broadcast the news. "Let's get this straight. You want to go poking around in the ground when we got skyscrapers to finish?"

"Yes."

"I have heard of this Jono."

"He's got Level 8 Health and Safety clearance."

"He does?" Mr Slater's eyes glint. It means Jono can fly even during rainfall; Arek only has Level 6. "Get the bloke to call me," says Mr Slater. "Not promising anything, mind."

Just after lunch, Jono calls Arek and says he *is* available. After giving out Mr Slater's number, Arek crosses his fingers.

When Arek hands in his afternoon worksheets Mr Slater says, "Looks like you got yourself a vote of reprieve. Blimey, the things you Floatas do for laughs."

"So you're taking Jono on?"

"Bloke sounds like he knows what's what. One condition, though."

"What?"

"Gotta tell everyone when you come back what it's like to make a prat of yourself in front of professors. We want details, my son! Details." He chortles.

Arek ignores the comment and feels a glow in his chest – he can go!

#

Two weeks on and Arek is wearing a hat to protect himself from the sun. His hands are dirty with soil. Together with Daisy, a student, he's in Trench 5, using a spatula and paint brush to carefully excavate bones. Daisy is slim with a blue t-shirt that says *Archaeologists Do It Underground* and dark hair like Em's, tied into a pony-tail.

"Arek. Look at this!" Daisy's meticulous excavation has revealed the top half of a bone. "I think this might be a Floata spinal vertebra."

The back of his neck tingles. "Oh, god. Really?"

"Grab that ID sheet, would you?" asks Daisy.

A laminated copy of illustrations of Floata spinal bones is weighted down by a small rock. Arek picks it up and hands it to her, staying close to get a good view. She smells of sweat and suncream. He looks back and forth from the illustration to the find, feeling a buzz of excitement,

"It is, isn't it? See how thick it is at that end, then narrows." Daisy indicates with a finger.

"Jesus. Yes!" A distant ancestor of his is right here in Trench 5. He sucks in a breath, presses his palms together.

"Stay there. I'm going to fetch Professor Lerner," says Daisy.

Heat radiates through Arek's chest as he continues to stare at the bone. He knows it's been speculated for decades that a small number of Floatas came as part of the Roman occupation of Britain – a minor reference to the 'fierce sky people' in Tactitus' *Annals* has sometimes been interpreted as meaning Floatas; but because Floata bones are lighter than those of humans – more akin to those of birds – they decay more easily and are rarely found. Floatas probably provided advance artillery in Roman times, shooting arrows from the air, striking terror and awe into the tribal areas being invaded.

Professor Lerner has a square, sunburnt face and deep-set, intelligent eyes. "My gosh," she says, and claps her hands together. "Definitely Floata bones. Only the third time I've ever seen these. Well done, you two, but don't touch anything for now. I'll get Heidi to take photos."

That evening, Arek sits with Daisy for dinner in the refectory along with a couple of other students from Daisy's university. They all chat about the finds that day, the most talkative being Olivia, a young woman with dyed blue hair, a posh accent and hands that chop the air as she talks. "You sound happy to have found Floata bones, Arek," she says. "Are you involved in Floata Rights Now?"

"No." Arek doesn't talk politics with people he doesn't know well, a habit picked up back home during The Troubles. "Work keeps me too busy."

"But you Floatas are treated badly here, like second class citizens. Jesus. Makes me livid. There was a lot in the press about that march last month. I so wanted to go but it was bloody exam week." Olivia's nose-ring glints as intensely as her eyes.

"Oh?" Arek doesn't really want to be drawn on the subject.

Olivia talks on about an article she read on discrimination against Floatas, glancing regularly at Arek, for approval or to gauge his reaction – he can't tell. He begins to feel irritated; she doesn't even ask him about his experience, even if he wouldn't discuss it with a stranger.

Daisy stands. "Looks like dessert is served. Anyone like some? Arek, come and help me?"

"Thanks for rescuing me," says Arek once they're out of earshot.

"Olivia's okay really. Fierce but okay."

He prefers people like Daisy who don't feel a need to fill a room with strong opinions. "It's a sensitive subject."

She meets his eye and nods, acknowledging his words. Then she indicates the dessert table. "Let's deal with the existential issue of: would you like chocolate fudge pudding or lemon cheesecake?"

After dessert Arek and Daisy sneak off alone to drink a beer outside her tent and listen to music on her iphone. "I like this one," says Arek as Coldplay's *Yellow* comes on.

"I like Coldplay too, though it'd be super uncool to admit that at uni."

"One thing I like about you – not hung up on being cool." This marks her out from some students here.

She grins and takes a swig of beer. He likes the angular line of her jaw and her cute, upturned nose.

"Do you ever feel resentful of the fact we're all studying at uni while you have to work?" she asks.

He turns the question over in his mind. If honest, he does – how he'd love to be studying full time – but he says, "Right now, I'm just happy to be here."

"I'm happy you're here, too." She holds his eye a moment, then glances down.

Is she inviting something? He isn't sure and is pleased anyway to have made a friend. He likes her more than is normal for him, but tells himself he wouldn't want to disappoint her – his last girlfriend, who barely lasted a couple of months, complained about him being aloof.

He and Daisy listen quietly to Coldplay as they finish their beer, and then, feeling awkward, he gets up, saying he really should go to bed.

She stares at her feet. "Okay."

He glances back as he walks away, but she has already vanished into the tent.

The sky holds a river of stars. How he'd love to whip up into it before bed. The only thing he misses about work is being allowed to fly.

#

On Arek's last day at the dig, Professor Lerner asks to see him. Her greying bobbed hair frames her face. "Enjoyed your time here?" she asks.

"Loved it."

"Everyone speaks highly of you and says you've been such an asset to the team." Professor Lerner's lithe arms move energetically as she speaks. "Someone told me you went on a dig in Mexico when a teenager."

41

"Yes, I did. Mayan ruins."

"And I gather you work now on a building site?"

He nods but the reminder of what awaits next week sinks his heart.

"Do you know about the Linneker Scholarships which fund Floatas who came here as refugees to do undergraduates degrees in London?" she asks.

"Yes, but you need three UniCerts or their equivalent, don't you? Because of work, it's taken me four years so far to get two. I got a Grade A for History but only a B for Biology."

"There are rare exemptions to the UniCert rule. Experience related to the degree, such as coming on a dig like this, would count, as would a reference from a relevant academic."

"Really? You're saying…"

"I'd be happy to write you a glowing reference." Her smile is warm. "It's obvious archaeology is your passion. Apply when you get home. With your two UniCerts, your digging experience and my reference, you've got an excellent chance."

Excitement flushes through him. "Oh, god. Thank you, Professor Lerner."

"And if you wanted to apply to UCL in London, where I'm based, even better."

He can hardly contain his excitement and has to stop himself from hugging her.

Later, after dinner, the youngsters are gathered round a campfire. Arek is sitting, watching the flames cast flickering shadows over the faces. His head still buzzes with the door to a future that Professor Lerner has opened for him, and he has downed enough beer to be fairly drunk. It's getting late, a full moon hangs in the sky, and they're playing a game. Going round clockwise, each person in turn has to stand and perform in some way. Daisy sings a Laura Marling song on her guitar. Olivia says she will recite Maya Angelou's poem *Caged Bird*. "The free bird floats on the back of the wind, um…" Her words are slurry. "Oh, shit. I'm too pissed to remember it."

Arek, up next, has no idea what to do. He drinks more beer to try to kill his nerves, but his throat goes dry as his turn comes.

"Arek! Arek!" chants Daisy, clapping her hands.

As Arek stands, his mind goes blank. Faces stare.

"Why not give us a flying demo?" says Daisy.

Arek shakes his head. He doesn't have a Flying Permit wristband and recreational flying is illegal.

"The law is draconian, it should be repealed," says Daisy. "None of us here will tell."

"Fly, fly!" others call.

Normally, he'd be adamant about not breaking the law, however much he disagrees with it, but being drunk, excited at his future and wanting to impress Daisy make him braver. "No one film it on your phone, okay?"

"Anyone try, I'll confiscate their phone," says Daisy.

Oh, to hell with it, he thinks. They are right out in the country here.

He stretches out his wings and whips up into the air, flapping hard until he's some way above the ground. The wind hisses in his ears, his breath comes rapidly.

He stops abruptly – he's showing off now, wasn't skydive champion back home four times for nothing – and hovers before diving vertically down, heading towards the campfire, wind in his face. Well before he reaches the fire, he loops upwards, pumps into the sky. His cheeks flush with pleasure as applause comes from below.

He darts in a figure of eight. Curls round and round in quick circles, hands tucked to his feet, before uncurling. Sweat prickles his skin. Whoops come from the onlookers.

He turns a somersault and plunges down dare-devil-style, his arms outstretched in front, holding his nerve. Just as heat from the campfire starts to prickle his fingertips, he arches his back, swoops up into the sky.

When did he last fly like this? What joy! What freedom! He hears clapping, but that no longer matters; what does is the thrill in his sinews, the tingling of his skin.

As soon as he lands, people mill round to offer praise. "That was so cool," gushes Olivia.

Feeling crowded, he moves away from them and the bonfire. His exhilaration is already segueing to worry. What if someone surreptitiously filmed him and posts it online?

"Hey," says a voice behind him.

He turns to see Daisy.

"You're quite the aerial acrobat," she says with a grin, then her expression clouds. "Are you okay?"

"No one filmed me, did they?"

"No. Don't worry. Both Olivia and I kept an eye out. No one here would do that anyway. They understand the risks."

Relief seeps through him.

She gets out a piece of yellow clothing from her bag and hands it to him. "Here, a parting gift. As you're going home tomorrow. One of mine but clean and newish and it'll fit."

He holds up a tee-shirt. On the front it says: *I found this humerus*, over a picture of an ancient humerus bone. He chuckles at the archaeological joke. "Thanks."

Neither of them speaks for a minute. He wants to tell her he's loved getting to know her, but being shy, the words catch in his throat and he ends up saying, "Well, I should be off to bed. I'm a bit pissed and got an early start."

She glances away. "Night, then."

He starts to walk away, wondering if he'll see her again.

She calls out, "We should meet up sometime when I get home from here. I'm in Reading so not that far from you."

He spins round, grinning ear to ear. "I'd love that."

The Job Lottery

I stride across Encorp Square, the tree-lined space in the city centre where the Lottery is held. I go past riot police, clowns on stilts, fire breathers, and stalls selling Prozac candy floss. EnCorp bills the Lottery as a public festival. "Festival? My arse," Ella would say. She isn't allowed to do the event this year – she's been diagnosed with Deviant Personality Disorder. The shrink says her condition is curable and she should be better in a year. As if.

It's a suitably overcast day. Outside EnCorp Guildhall, an ugly grey building, the crowd thickens and I elbow my way up the steps and go through a main door. Inside, within the spacious lobby, stand the rows of Entrance Kiosks, each made of metal and the size of a small shed. Pictures of a smiling President Morrow-Rudd decorate their sides, lots of people stand in queues in front. The people don't seem real, but then nothing about the Lottery does – it's like watching a crap Channel 55 sci-fi film directed by a sociopath.

As I join the shortest queue, I break into a sweat. The newspaper held by the man in front of me has the headline: *Extremists Demand Wage Rise and Free PsychoBliss Drops*. Who believes this bullshit? I text Ella: *At Guildhall. Waiting to go in.*

She replies: *Sod EnCorp! And we're out of caffeinated ice-cream.*

I drum irritably on my left thigh with my fingers, a habit she dislikes. She didn't even wish me luck before I left this morning, and I have to provide for us both.

After about ten minutes of waiting, my palms getting stickier, my turn comes. Steeling myself, I walk into the Entrance Kiosk. The metal door slides closed behind me; there's a smell of stale sweat and broken dreams. At the desk, the thin, female EnCorp official in a red uniform scans my ID card into the computer. "Anything to declare, Miss Fisher?" she asks.

From the inner pocket of my coat, I fish out a gold ring – Mum's wedding band, which Dad wanted me to have. I didn't tell Ella I was bringing it, she'd have stopped me. But what else do I have? As I hold out the ring, I silently curse the Lottery. The official's gaze darts nervously towards the door before she pockets it.

"Tell me now, please," I say quietly.

She leans towards me. "Choose pink. Higher numbers better," she whispers.

From her face, I've no idea if she's lying. Bribing EnCorp officials always carries a risk.

She returns my ID card and gestures to the exit door. "Go through. Only fifteen minutes by the pool or you lose your choice."

Choice? What bullshit!

In the vast, rectangular hall, a banner hanging from the ceiling reads, *EnCorp Wishes You a Good Lottery — Seize the Moment!* Fancy kidding myself I'm in control. Dad, who grew up in the time before EnCorp, can't get his head round the Lottery. Mind you, from what I've read, having a choice of work back then wasn't all it was cracked up to be either, at least not for plebs like us.

My gut churns as I walk across the hall. EnCorp changes the way the Lottery is done each year, supposedly making it 'fun' — last year we chased numbered guinea pigs, and two years ago we had to search for coloured ping-pong balls in a mountain of sand. This year a huge yellow paddling-pool of water stands at the hall's centre; on the surface are thousands of plastic ducks — red, blue, green, yellow, pink, and white ones. I grab a butterfly net from a basket that contains dozens of them, and head straight to the poolside. People are snatching frantically at the ducks with the nets, while mean-eyed security guards with batons watch over proceedings.

A gaunt man with bloodshot eyes hurls his net into the pool in frustration. "This is ridiculous," he shouts. He is quickly bundled away by security guards to a Public Penance Trampoline. A dozen trampolines are in the hall, all of them in use. Last year Ella had to bounce for telling a security guard where to shove the Lottery. She finds it hard to keep her mouth shut — that's the difference between us.

One woman bouncing on a Public Penance Trampoline wears a blue cassock which billows and shrinks like a swimming jellyfish as she goes up and down. She speaks through a loud-hailer. "We're not worthy." Bounce. "Need to better ourselves." Bounce. "Work hard." Bounce. "Work sets us free." Bounce.

A shiver runs down my back. She *must* be a PR bod for EnCorp.

To my right, two middle-aged women both have hold of a purple duck. "Give it me," hisses one. "Mine, you bitch," spits the other. They are dragged away by security guards. "Please. No. It's all *her* fault," wails the first.

Nothing that happens in this dumb Lottery surprises me.

I stand by the pool attempting to hook ducks with my butterfly net. Next to me is a bloke simply staring at the water. "Is life a lottery?" he says to no one in particular.

If it is, the game is rigged – at least for poor people like us.

I manage to net three pink ducks, and hope the tip I got from the thin official earlier is accurate. I check which duck is labelled with the highest number, hold on to that, and chuck the others back in the pool. After dumping the butterfly net in another basket, I queue at an Exit Kiosk. The grey-haired woman in front of me clenches her red duck tightly to her chest. I move my pink one fretfully from one hand to the other, praying the job I get will be okay.

In the Exit Kiosk, a male official in a red uniform takes my duck, taps its number into his computer, and prints a small Job Allocation Card.

"What job is it?" I cross my fingers.

"I've seen a lot worse." He hands me the card.

Without reading it, I hurry outside, where the sky is clearing, the sun coming out. Endgame Square, a large, concrete space, is full of people who've done the Lottery. A few of them are celebrating, but many sit looking dejected, or try to swap jobs with one other, flashing their cards. A public tannoy system is playing *We're All Monday's Heroes*. God, I hate that song.

With bated breath, I read my Job Card: five ten-hour night-shifts a week as a Senior Warehouse Supervisor at the EnCorp Knitting Emporium. Nights aren't great – travel can be dangerous then – but it's regular work and the money will cover all our basics and the occasional emergency. Working nights, I'll get plenty of time to read, too. Handing over Mum's ring was worthwhile. I allow myself a smile.

Without Ella, I'd actually manage okay on this money, even be able to visit Dad up North once a year and have luxuries sometimes – a bottle of Alcoheaven, a chocolate Munchbomb. But why am I thinking this? Ella has no one else. No. One. Else.

How will she handle me being gone most nights? She woke shouting from a nightmare at 3am again last night. "S'okay," I said, stroking her hair. "Just a dream."

I better get going and tell her about the job.

A teenage girl who can't be much more than sixteen approaches me. "Wanna swap? The money's good," she says. Her eyes are pensive and her purple lipstick smudged.

"What have you got?" It can't hurt to find out.

"City prostitute."

"Behind EnCorp Head Office?"

Grimacing, she nods.

Poor kid. The elite there are sadists. "What's the pay?" I ask.

"Two thou' a month." She shows me her card.

Could I do it? On that money Ella and I'd be able to save up quite a bit, maybe even get out of the city in a year's time. She'd hate me doing it, though. "You can't sleep with those bastards," she'd say, "they screw us enough as it is." She's right, of course, and there'd be the medical bills for antibiotics and stitches.

"Sorry, no," I say. "Is this your first lottery?"

"Ner, I'm seventeen." Her chin juts up. "Gotta find a swap."

"You will. Keep asking around." I hope she finds someone more desperate than me.

As I walk away, I glance round Endgame Square. The atmosphere is tense – stalls doing a bustling trade in Mogadon smoothies and Prozac candy floss, cards being torn up, fights breaking out, security guards and riot police muscling in. About a dozen Public Penance Trampolines are in use, and spectators hurl things at the bouncers – insults, apple cores, plastic ducks. There'll be a riot soon. Always is. For years I hung around because I found the riot cathartic, but now I have Ella to think of, so I join the stream leaving the square.

I briefly pause on Adcart Bridge to look over the side. Sunlight quivers in diamonds on the river's surface; water comforts me, I'm not sure why. A muscular bloke in a tight, white tee-shirt, probably an undercover policeman, stops next to me and gives me the eye. "Done the Lottery?" he asks.

I nod, but my shoulders tense.

"You could do with some fun, then." His black-slug eyebrows rise up. "I know a cheap PleasureDome near here."

"I'm meeting my husband any minute." Sometimes lying like this works with his sort.

"So what." He grabs my wrist.

I try to pull away. "Let go. Please."

He holds fast and the passers-by all look the other way. "Come on, blondie. You know you want it."

My wrist is starting to hurt. "Get the hell off me," I shout.

He lets go, but then spits in my face. "Stupid tart! Too skinny for me anyway."

I scurry away, my heart thrumming. I glance back to check he isn't following, then wipe his spit off my face with my sleeve. God, men can be so disgusting.

My pulse has just about returned to normal by the time I enter the frozen food warehouse on Mercy Street. I hope they still sell ice-cream – last week the bakery next-door was only selling second-hand laptops, tinned fruit and recycled teddy bears. I'm relieved to find a freezer full of caffeinated ice-cream, Ella's favourite, and buy two large tubs. I try to make her eat healthily, but she just turns her pretty nose up. "Who cares what I eat?" she says.

"You're on medication. You need something healthy."

"Bugger that."

"You'll get fat."

"I'm fat already. You like fat women."

True, I do.

As I leave the warehouse, I notice people running down the street. A few seconds later a riot policeman hurtles by, too. "Stop or I'll shoot!" he yells, then fires a shot without bothering to wait. A woman ahead squeals and falls to the ground, clutching at her leg. Shit! A siren goes off in the distance and my pulse races. It's time I got well away.

Just past Cheapskates, I nip right into Fortune Place where anxious-looking shop-keepers are pulling down metal grates on shop-fronts. I dash down the narrow alley beside Budget Drugs – or Budget Drudge as Ella calls it. You have to know the area well to know this cut-through; Ella worked in that shop for a year. Ahead of me are two women and, hearing my fast footsteps behind them, they look back nervously. I wave to show I'm friendly and they nod to acknowledge me. We all hurry to the end, coming out in Darkhorse Lane, where there's hardly anyone about. Phew! I should be okay from here.

Forty minutes' walk brings me home to Worn Road, which has more potholes than tarmac. Halfway down, I stop abruptly. In the decaying oak are two parrots with crimson plumage. I've seen parrots here before, but not like this and not for ages. Something beautiful, something unexpected, exists after all. I smile and shake my head before setting off.

The stairwell in our four-storey, red-brick block stinks of mould and pee. Ella and I want to move from here, but it's difficult to do – a thousand quid to bribe officials for a Flat Move Visa.

As I open the front door of our second floor flat, I call out, "Hey."

No answer. I check the small flat, walking quickly room to room. There's piles of mess everywhere but no Ella. Where the hell is she? She rarely goes out alone, but maybe she's popped to the local shops? I rinse out one of the dirty mugs in the kitchen sink, and make myself a cup of tea to drink while waiting. *Come on, hurry up, Ella*, I think.

After half an hour has passed, I text her, but there's no reply. Where can she be? I do all the washing up, then pace the room. I try to sit and read my book. Can't concentrate. A troubling idea flies to me and I rush to the bathroom cabinet, get out her pills, check how many there are. Thank god almost all are here still; I picked up her prescription a few days ago. She's never taken an overdose, but I guess you never know, and the suicide rate always spikes on Lottery day. My relief is brief, though, and I pace the flat once more.

An hour later, the front door opens.

"Hey," says Ella, and closes the door behind her. She's in baggy jeans and a denim jacket, and her long, brown hair is tugged into a bun, a few stray strands framing her wide, pretty face.

"Where the hell have you been?" I ask.

"For Christ sake. Keep your hair on, woman."

"I thought you'd be waiting to find out about my job," I say curtly.

She frowns. "Is the job… shit?"

"Actually, the money's okay. Look!" I hand her my card.

She holds it, staring, and then glances up. "Nights."

"I know they're your bad times."

"I'm more worried about *you* travelling actually, but this money *is* okay." There is a flicker of a smile on her face as she hands me the card back.

"I got caffeinated ice-cream, too."

"Thanks, honey. I've got something to show you as well." From her pocket, she produces a Job Card and holds it out.

Surprised, I grab it and read. It's for regular reception work at Pluto's Tombstone Warehouse. Decent money. "But how the hell did you get this?" I ask. Like I said, she's on the Prohibited From Work list

"I did the Lottery." She shows me a fake ID – her photo but in the name of Emma Fischer.

"Where on earth…?"

"There *are* ways to game the system." She pats herself playfully on the chest, then lets out a breath. "Well, I pawned Gran's gold necklace to get it."

"But the shrink's report—"

"That can piss right off. The moron just couldn't handle the fact I'm smart and have attitude."

Ella has bravado; underneath she's vulnerable, too. "What about the anti-deviancy therapy?" I ask.

She screws up her nose. "I can do that crap Tuesday evenings."

"It's dangerous. EnCorp might rumble you."

"They're bastards, but incompetent bastards."

She's right about them being incompetent, but I still feel uneasy.

She opens up her palms. "Being cooped up here doing bugger all's driving me nuts. It's worse than a shit job. Can't you see?"

"What if you mouth off again and get in more trouble?"

"I *have* to learn to control my gob or we may not survive." Her face is both feisty and fragile. "With both our pay cheques, we'll be able to save up, maybe even get out of the city before you turn thirty. Rent ourselves a little flat by the sea up North near your dad. Wouldn't that be great? Maybe your dad can help us get jobs on the boats." There's a glint in her big brown eyes and her lips curl into that playful grin.

It is a smile that swells my heart, makes life seem real and tender. "Come here, Emma Fischer," I say.

Her arms reach out as she steps towards me.

Knitting to Oblivion

Joss woke with a sense something was wrong. The blackbirds and tits, which brought song to her morning, were silent. She got up, padded out to the landing, and peered from the window at her back garden. *It's not there,* she thought. The stone birdbath, which had stood halfway down her short garden, seemed to be gone. She threw on clothes to hand, an ironed cord skirt and wool sweater, and rushed downstairs.

In the kitchen sat Asha, the lodger. Her black hair, with a few grey strands, fell to her shoulders and she was in pyjamas, knitting her long, purple scarf. Asha didn't bother looking up; she seemed permanently tuned out of the world and into something interior.

Joss pressed her nose up to the window. "Christ," she exclaimed.

"What?" said Asha.

Joss pointed. "My birdbath's vanished." As she opened the back door, a cool shot of spring air greeted her. She stared: the object was nowhere to be seen. "Where the hell's it gone?"

"Dunno," said Asha. "Things do that – go."

"Not cemented-down birdbaths." Joss's gaze darted around the garden. Could thieves have taken it? The six-foot fence was undamaged and the only way into the garden was through the house. She stepped outside onto the patio to check she wasn't missing anything, but no, there was no birdbath.

Back inside, Joss said, "How on earth did someone manage to steal it?"

"Maybe it just, you know, vanished."

"Things don't just vanish."

"Damn," said Asha. "Dropped a stitch."

Was Asha's attitude laid back or laid to rest? "You may not care, Asha. I liked watching the birds."

"The cats next-door did, too."

"They're not suspects then?"

"Pardon?"

"Never mind." When Joss phoned the police to report the incident, a voice told her she was ninth in the call queue. She hung up in frustration, promising herself to try again.

Asha was still focused on the purple scarf. Joss didn't understand the current craze for knitting though it wasn't quite as annoying as the crochet mania of last year. "Why do you knit all the time?" Joss asked.

Her thin face pinched in concentration, Asha said, "As a kinda antidote."

"To what?"

"All the unravelling."

"All what unravelling?"

Asha's big brown eyes stared past Joss. "I'm not sure you see."

"I'm afraid I don't."

Needing to get on, Joss had breakfast, washed up, and wiped the surfaces, stopping to check the labels on the tea and coffee jars were aligned. In the bathroom she put on foundation and plum lipstick, and tugged her long, thick, dark hair into a pony-tail. She frowned at her reflection, at the fine crows-feet round her green eyes. How had she got to the age of thirty-six? The last few years had flown as fast as a Boeing 747.

In the hallway she put on her long suede boots and *Mulberry* woollen coat. Going to the Job Centre never filled her with enthusiasm. In truth, she felt shame about being unemployed and deflected 'what do you do?' from strangers by firing some other question back. A woman of her education and work experience having to sign on, not to mention live on the paltry sum. So much for the Brexit sunlit uplands.

At the Hythe Road bus stop was one of Joss's neighbours, the plump, good-natured, grey-haired Mrs Anderson who was seated, knitting something long and royal blue.

Mrs Anderson's round face broke into a smile. "Morning, Joss."

"Morning, Mrs A. How are you?"

"Mustn't complain."

"You... don't knit as some sort of antidote, do you?"

Mrs Anderson screwed up her face into a frown. "Not sure what you mean, love. I knit cos it takes me mind off things." Mrs Anderson stared past Joss, her eyes growing wider. "Good lord!" She put her knitting on her lap and pointed a stubby finger to the opposite side of the road. "That old post-box has gone, the one what used to be there."

Joss spun around and then squinted: where the post-box had stood seemed to be a grey space, almost a hazy hole, which merged at its edges with the drab light of the morning. "How odd."

"They never nicked that, too," said Mrs Anderson.

"Who? Nicked what?"

"That gang of thieves what's been nicking stuff in town. Took that huge sculpture thing in the park yesterday. Was on Anglia News last night."

Joss hadn't seen the news, and her shoulders tensed as she recalled her vanishing birdbath. "A post-box would be very hard to nick."

"I'll phone the police later," said Mrs Anderson, turning back to her knitting. "Someone should tell 'em it's gone."

On board the bus, Joss sat next to Mrs Anderson and had to lean a bit towards the aisle to avoid the older woman's elbow as she knitted. Joss kept twisting her head left and right, keeping an eye out for anything else odd along the street.

"You'll dislocate your 'ed if you keep doing that," said Mrs Anderson.

"Aren't you worried about that missing post-box?"

"Oops," said Mrs Anderson. "Dropped me ball of wool. Couldn't pick it up, could you? Back's giving me jip."

Joss rescued it from the floor. After carefully wiping off the flecks of dirt, she handed it back, and noticed all Mrs Anderson's nails were bitten to the quick.

"Ta, love," said Mrs Anderson.

Joss didn't know the woman well – they exchanged pleasantries if they met in the street, nothing more – but was fond of her. Joss had never taken her as an anxious, nail-biting type.

Mrs Anderson got off at the Knitting Emporium, saying goodbye. Joss got off two stops later opposite the Job Centre. Now here was something Joss wished *would* vanish. Shame flushed through her as she crossed the road and pushed through the door.

Inside, she was called to a desk where a thin Job Centre Advisor she didn't recognise sat knitting something long and crimson. Joss was surprised he was allowed to do so at work. Still knitting, he asked about her job search. She told him she'd applied for fifteen jobs this last fortnight, with no luck.

"Hmm. Widen your search."

"I already have." She sighed. "Jobs like shop assistant or waiter won't often consider me. I'm way overqualified, they say."

He put down his knitting, and with a stern expression, typed into the computer. "You *must* still apply for those jobs."

"I do," she said through clenched teeth, hating the way certain advisors treated her as unmotivated or an idiot. "It'll be on the computer."

"How long have you been unemployed now?"

"Four months," she said. "But—"

"Sign the form," he interrupted, staring at her. "Then go to the computers and look for more jobs."

Irritated, she scribbled a signature, stood brusquely, and went over to a free computer. When she'd lost her old job at the Spanish translation agency, she'd never expected to find it difficult to get a new one, not with a degree in Spanish, eight years teaching experience, and several years working as a translator. *Damn the recession!*

She stayed on the computer for two hours, drumming her slim fingers as she scrolled through online ads, most for low-paid, low-skill jobs. She completed three job application forms. *Oh, to hell with this*, she thought eventually.

She decided to walk the three miles home to save herself the bus fare; penny pinching was a new and tedious experience. Along High Street she turned her face away to avoid looking at The Bridal Boutique; a memory of Pablo came anyway, but she pushed it back before it could take hold. The day was now clear and crisp, so she headed into Castle Park, taking a long pathway lined with trees, mainly lime and cherry. She sniffed the air, she loved the spring, although – look! – the magnolia tree had already lost its flowers.

Joss strolled beside the river, which carried reflections of cumulus clouds like sunken islands. She crossed Miller's Bridge, arched in surprise over the river, and then she stopped abruptly. A shiver ran across her shoulders – "No way!"

"Gone," said a man with white tufts of hair, who sat on a bench knitting something long and yellow. "Been there since about 1800."

"Where the hell's it gone?" The huge ancient oak at the top of the riverbank was missing. It wasn't like the tree had been cut down; there was an eerie space, like some existential rubber had erased it.

"Who knows? Trees vanish all the time in the Amazon, but you don't expect it to happen here."

Joss pressed her hands to her face. "This is weird."

"Try not to fret, dear."

"You're not worried?"

He shrugged and then looked at his knitting. "Oops. Dropped a stitch."

Joss strode off, her forceful steps suppressing the anxiety rising within her. What the hell was going on?

Asha was still knitting in the kitchen – she was often home during the day, being on a zero-hour contract. Now she wore a long, black skirt and a home-knitted purple jumper with matching fingerless gloves. Joss thought of her general dress-sense as 'frumpy, middle-aged goth'.

"That huge oak at Miller's Bridge has disappeared." Joss rubbed at her neck. "Poof! Gone!"

Asha barely glanced up. "Oh," she said flatly.

"Maybe... maybe it went the same way as my birdbath?"

Asha studied Joss with large eyes underscored by dark rings. "I think you need chamomile tea and chill-out music, Joss."

"No, I need to know why things are disappearing." Joss could hear the pitch of her voice rising. "There's the birdbath, the oak. The post-box in Hythe Road, too. All gone."

Asha looked down at her knitting. "Damn. Dropped a stitch."

"For Christ sake," snapped Joss. "What if, say, this cottage is next to vanish?"

When Asha shrugged, Joss felt like shaking her.

Trying to calm her nerves, Joss made herself a sandwich and cup of tea and had her lunch. Then, needing privacy, she shut herself in her bedroom and checked local radio news. There was nothing about disappearances on it, only loose claims about thieves stealing large objects in town. She wanted to search the net, but she'd sold her laptop to pay the last fuel bill and had run out of free web access on her phone this month. *Damn.* She thought of calling her mum, whom she was close to, but didn't want to worry her. Taking hold of her pony-tail, she wrapped its end round and round her finger, a habit she found soothing.

The spring light sluicing through the window only darkened her mood. Her attention was drawn to the gap on the windowsill where a favourite photo used to sit of her and Pablo, her ex fiancée: both smiling, hand-in-hand, outside the Guggenheim Museum, Bilbao; she'd shoved the photo in a cupboard three months ago, after he'd announced he was leaving her for an old girlfriend he'd reconnected with on Facebook. Even the gap perturbed her today, as if hinting at a gloomy truth. She twisted her gaze away, refusing to let herself dwell on all that now.

It was 2pm. She cleaned the upstairs bathroom until it shone, did the ironing, and tidied her room. Ticked those things off her to-do list. Lay on her bed with an mp3 player, choosing Eric Satie – calm and restrained. Picked up her novel, a thriller, and read for a while, but tired through stress, she eventually drifted into an uneasy sleep.

Joss woke to a cold room coloured by dusk. She rose and glanced out the window. "Jesus!" Her stomach tightened into a knot. Cynthia Bunyan's cottage – a Victorian terraced one similar to hers, on the other side – was gone, as was the cherry tree in front. She could just make out the large, shadowy space under the hibiscus-orange streetlight.

Downstairs, Asha was still knitting. "Cynthia Bunyan's house…" said Joss.

Asha frowned. "Disappeared?"

Joss nodded. They slunk outside together and stared at the space, a ghostly gap in the material of the world. Joss's heart banged in her chest.

"Shit." Asha scratched at her arm.

"You're worried now?"

"More like interested."

"Interested?"

"Nebulous disappearances, possible or actual oblivion. Interesting."

"Sometimes I think you're mad."

"Sometimes I think I'm sane."

Joss pointed a nervous finger toward the empty space. "Think Cynthia was in it when it went?"

"No. That woman never gets home til late. Usually drunk."

Joss looked up and down the road, her stomach still tense. At this time, it was usually busy with people returning home from work. "Why's no one around?"

"Dunno. Strange."

"What shall we do?"

Asha's eyes narrowed. "My intuition tells me: go inside and knit."

"Are you serious? Let's talk to Heather." Joss strode over and knocked loudly on her next-door neighbour's door. A light was on, but there was no answer. "Heather?" she shouted through the letter-box. When no response came, she shivered.

"Come inside, Joss," called Asha.

Joss did so, shutting the front door brusquely behind her.

Asha stared at her mobile. "Jesus. I've got no signal whatsoever. Try your phone."

Joss picked up her mobile – same problem, and she had no landline. Desperate for information, she flicked on local radio news; there was only a feature about hedgehog decline. *News 24* on the television was covering the recession caused by Brexit, *ITV News* the refugee crisis in the Mediterranean. Joss put a hand to her temple; her mind felt so jumbled. A disturbing thought, an insight, pressed at her, but she couldn't grasp its measure fully. She shook it off. "Come on. Let's walk into town."

"No," said Asha firmly. "We do that tomorrow if need be, when it's light. For now we stay put, keep an eye on the news, and distract ourselves – knit."

"For god's sake. I don't even know how to knit."

"Time you learned."

"Never going to happen."

Asha pondered a moment. "We could play Scrabble."

"Scrabble?"

"It'll distract you and make you feel better. You always thrash me."

63

Joss hesitated, and then nodded. Why not? She had no better idea. She turned down the volume on *News 24,* and they set up the Scrabble on the table.

Joss drew her first seven letters. "Oh, shit, I've got: AWL GONE." The words hurt, as if slicing open a wound within.

"Well, I've got AGH HOPE," said Asha.

Asha, who continued knitting whenever it was Joss's turn, began to win by a larger and larger margin. "For Christ's sake. Concentrate, Joss."

Normally competitive at any games, Joss couldn't focus at all. She pressed her palm to her brow. "But my head keeps asking – what... why... how the hell..."

"Three good questions."

"To which there are answers?"

"Are there ever answers?"

Joss curbed her urge to slap Asha who seemed too knowing to know anything.

Asha's bony hands slid back and forth, back and forth, looping wool with a finger over one needle, using the other needle to create each new stitch. Joss found herself staring: it was a consoling rhythm and Joss needed consolation, being deeply troubled by the disappearances. No, not solely by them. By something still deeper and even more encompassing, too. "Maybe you were right, Asha."

"About what?"

Joss frowned, trying to clarify what was in her head. "I don't really see, do I?"

"Who does?"

"You do. You saw something coming, didn't you? You talked about things unravelling."

"I've felt something unravelling for a time, but assumed it was me. I honestly didn't care about the birdbath or oak tree at first. I..." Asha's forehead creased as if she was struggling for words. "They didn't seem important. I guess...I was just too preoccupied with myself."

A realisation hit Joss like a blow to the head, something it took courage to admit. "I think I've been unravelling, too."

Asha raised a black eyebrow. "Seriously? You always seem so organised and together to me."

Those words used to be fitting, but Joss felt distant and alien from them now. "I think I'm good at pretending, good at denial."

"Aren't we all." Asha looked tenderly at Joss.

Joss glanced away, her eyes coming to rest on a framed Dali poster on the wall – on its melting clocks and deserted beach overcast by dark shadows. She felt grief push up towards her throat and closed her eyes tight to hold back the tears. She took a deep breath to compose herself and opened her lids. "Why've you been unravelling, Asha?"

Asha stopped knitting and rubbed her chest with one hand. "I'm forty," she said. "I'm not... Life's not... Well, it's a long story."

"Want to tell me? We've got all night."

A shadow flitted across Asha's eyes. "We *hope* we've got all night. Do you think..."

An icy feeling gripped Joss. "Let's try not to think too much," she said. "I'm hungry. Let's eat something."

They gave up on Scrabble and together prepared a dinner of bacon omelette with new potatoes and French beans, which tasted good, comforting. They ate listening to local radio and the lack of mention of objects disappearing unsettled Joss once again.

After washing up, Joss went outside to see if she could get a phone signal in Hythe Road. No luck. *Damn.* She wanted to call her mum and just hoped the woman was okay – surely this wasn't happening up in Leeds, too. Trying to avoid looking at the gap opposite, Joss glanced up and down the street. Still no one around. Why not? Her skin prickling with fear, she hurried back inside.

In the living room, Joss sat flicking through television channels, watching one programme for ten minutes, then another. Asha simply knitted on and on, the clicking of her needles a subdued percussion.

"Don't take this the wrong way: shall we sleep in the same bed tonight?" said Joss eventually.

"Why not."

They decided not to change into nightclothes. In bed, Asha drifted off to sleep quickly, while Joss struggled to do so. Where Asha's sleeve had ridden up, there was a little tattoo of a compass on her inner arm. Joss felt a swell of tenderness: her lodger, a lost woman with a compass tattoo.

I'm lost, too. That thought was almost overwhelming. Tears stung Joss's eyes. She let herself cry, but quietly so as not to wake Asha.

A troubled sleep finally overcame her. Threads of dreams showed her oak trees and post-boxes tossed about stormy skies.

She woke to loud honking. Asha was by the window, early morning sunlight blanching her face. "Something's up," said Asha.

Joss jumped out of bed. As she looked from the window, her hands trembled. Two more terraced houses opposite were gone, though thankfully there were more people about. In fact, a traffic jam had formed up Hythe Road. People leapt out of the cars; some gesticulated wildly, others sat on their bonnets knitting furiously.

"Something is definitely up," said Joss.

In the kitchen downstairs, Joss gulped down a glass of water. She put on boots and a coat and shot outside with Asha who was holding tight to her knitting. Joss asked someone passing: "What's happening?"

The woman was pale, breathless. "Saint Botolph's roundabout... top of road... vanished... Brook Street and Regent Street... gone too."

"Christ!" exclaimed Joss. "Is the rail station still there?"

"Dunno... I'm running out of town however I can... Do the same. Run!" She dashed away.

"Joss?" murmured Asha.

Jumbled thoughts cluttered Joss's mind. "I need to see the missing roundabout for myself, Ash. Not sure why. Come with me?"

Asha nodded. "Let's stay together." She checked her mobile phone. "Shit! Still no signal."

They hurried the half kilometre down Hythe Road, passing some house-sized voids – holes in the fraying fabric of the world. Knitted objects were strewn about: an enormous cerise flower on a tree branch, a large, yellow bobble hat over a post-box, a green blanket dotted with white daisies on a driveway.

"All this knitting," said Asha. "Putting things back into the world."

Joss scoffed. "Like knitting's going to stop an apocalypse."

Where St Botolphs's roundabout had once stood was now a round mound of nothing. A crowd of people was gathered; nervous murmurings rumbled through it and one young man frenetically knitted something large and grey. Signs were held high: *Repent: The End is Nigh, Half Price Whiskey at The Anchor Now.*

A shiver sped down Joss's spine. "Let's go home, grab some stuff, get away from this nightmare."

Asha, her face deathly pale, agreed.

On the way back, Joss looked in shock at the spectral space that used to be St Helen's Lane, the only side-street off Hythe Road; she'd loved that little cobbled cut-through street and felt a surge of sadness. Further down, half a dozen people were huddled in a group by the side of the road. Two rocked back and forth, sobbing; the others sat on the tarmac in a circle, knitting something large and brick-red, each working from one side. Joss's heart warmed a little as she recognised one of them. "Mrs A!"

The woman looked up. "Joss," she exclaimed. "Oh, my god. I thought you'd…"

"What?"

"Disappeared with your house."

Joss's heart lurched. Her precious home, the one constant in the last months of turmoil, was gone? Surely that couldn't be for good – such horror was too huge to fathom. She made herself focus on Mrs A instead. "What about your house?"

Mrs Anderson looked about to cry. "Gone, too."

"Christ," Joss whimpered. "Come on! Let's get out of here."

"But Church Street roundabout at the top has gone, like Saint Botolph's."

Joss swallowed with a hard gulp. "You mean… we're trapped?"

Mrs Anderson nodded.

"Why the hell are you knitting?" Joss burst out.

"Gotta do something." Mrs Anderson gestured to the knitted object. "We're making a house. Then we'll make another and another. See?"

"Not sure I do."

As Mrs Anderson began to cry, Joss's heart went out to her. "Sorry. I didn't mean to upset you, Mrs A."

"You're the least of my problems, love."

"Let's go," whispered Asha.

They said a quick, poignant goodbye and continued down Hythe

Road. There were haunting gaps where houses had once stood, like absences in reality; there were clusters of frightened people, some knitting urgently; and there were shrieks and sobs, but beyond that only a strange silence. As they snaked round each group of people, Joss wasn't sure where they were going or why. She made herself put one foot in front of the other, a fluid fear seeping into her. "There's nothing back there... and nothing ahead of us."

"Sounds like life," said Asha.

Joss shot her a look of disgust. "Stop being so philosophical! I'm terrified. We need to bloody get out of here."

Halting, Asha tipped her head up at the dark clouds swathing the sky in gloom, then after a minute or so, spoke in a determined tone. "To hell with it! I think we should just walk straight into the void."

"Are you insane?"

"Got any better ideas?"

"Has to be some other way."

"Join the knitters?"

Joss glanced angrily at Asha.

"What if the gaps in the world are connected to the unravelling we feel inside?" said Asha.

"Don't be crazy," said Joss. "This isn't just happening to us, but to the whole bloody town."

"What if this is only *actually* happening to those of us aware that holes exist, in ourselves, in the world?"

All this scary shit was just one big concrete or manifesting metaphor? "That sounds ridiculous."

"I know. But isn't it all we've got?"

Didn't Asha have a point? Disjointed thoughts whirled through Joss's mind; she pressed fingers to her skull to try and stop them. Only one thing was certain in the chaos, she realised — courage was needed. She summoned strength. "Okay. Let's walk."

Asha tossed her knitting defiantly into the gutter and offered a cold, sweaty hand to Joss. Hand-in-hand, they took a few steps forward.

Joss's mouth fell open in fright, in awe as she stared up at the great nothingness ahead, which billowed and shape-shifted — now a huge, man-shaped hollow, now a giant tree of nothingness, now a coffin-shaped tower of zilch. Her heart hammered so loud she could hear it in her ears.

Asha halted. "Oh God," she whimpered.

"Come on! Be brave."

"Maybe... we're making a mistake."

A phrase flew to Joss, she was unsure from where. "On the other side of nothing, there's a better world." Saying it aloud induced in her an odd composure.

"You really think?"

"There has to be."

The Colour of Dulton

Thomas P. Mockchild wasn't a popular man, even though he – or rather his body – served public functions in the small town of Dulton. Being publicly useful wasn't something he chose. It was an indirect consequence of the mysterious affliction he suffered from – he could sleep on public benches for days at a time, sometimes for more than a week. While asleep he sat as upright as a lamp-post and seemed as tranquil as a monk.

Thomas was eighteen when the affliction began; he was spotted sleeping on the bench outside Dulton library. Passers-by and librarians couldn't fail to hear his snores, like those of a hibernating bear, and after a few hours, the police were called. Unable to rouse the young man, they carted him off to hospital. There, no doctor could awaken him, not even, as was eventually tried, with sharp needles or loud hollering. After a battery of medical tests, followed by a session of technical head-scratching, the doctors pronounced him fit to go home: he wasn't punch-drunk or in a coma, they concluded, but in a sleep of such depth that he could have been an elderly sloth. The police took him back to the bedsit where he lived alone and tucked him under his duvet. But the next day he was again found sitting asleep on the library bench, his tattooed hands balanced in his lap.

No one could remember exactly when 'Sleeping Thomas' had first been put to public use. Some said it'd been when the library was refurbished and the sign explaining this had somehow been left on his lap; others said it'd been over Christmas when, to blend Sleeping Thomas in with the town's decorations, he'd been dressed up as Santa. Soon, it was tacitly, if not officially, acknowledged that his somnambulant body could be used for a variety of social and business ventures. Each year the 'Dulton in Bloom' committee placed a tub of petunias in his hands, matching the hanging baskets along High Street. And businesses left signs around his neck or on his lap: *Half-Price Cupcakes Today at The Nice Café, Happy Hour 6-7pm at The OddFellow Arms.*

#

Rose Johanssen, the new assistant at the library, glanced out of the window at a pale leaden sky. Was Dulton *always* grey? As the library door swung open for a customer, her attention was drawn to a sound coming from High Street, like the snores of a drunk. "What's that noise?" she asked the senior librarian, Noel Trapise.

"Oh, just Sleeping Thomas." Noel was a forty-something, conscientious man with a slight pouch on an otherwise bony frame.

"Sorry. Who?"

He took off his small, metal-framed glasses and wiped them with a cloth. "I forgot you're new to town. The chap who sleeps on public benches."

"He's homeless?"

"No." He explained that Thomas had a strange disorder and slept in public, sometimes for over a week.

Rose glanced down, Noel must be pulling her leg. She wondered again if it'd been wise to move to Dulton from her parents' home an hour's drive away. At twenty-one, even if shy, she was surely old enough to fly the nest.

Putting his glasses back on, Noel peered at her from under bushy black eyebrows. "Not heard of Sleeping Thomas?"

"I'm afraid not." Rose was too ashamed to admit she hadn't had any proper conversations during her first fortnight in town; she found it hard to make friends.

"Why not see for yourself at lunchtime?"

On lunch break, Rose went out to the public bench and saw Thomas: a slender young man in a khaki parka, his eyes closed. He had a thin face, ginger stubble and disheveled shoulder-length hair, and was sitting upright like a dancer but snoring like a bear. Something odd – A5 sized and on a cord – hung round his neck, but she couldn't see it clearly at this distance. Passers-by began to stare at her, so she ducked into the newsagent and bought a *Mars Bar*. Rose asked about Sleeping Thomas.

"A malingerer. All that sleeping keeps the scrounger on benefits," said the shop-keeper.

"Well, I heard he's got a serious sleeping disorder," Rose said before striding out. Quite how protective she felt towards this scruffy stranger surprised her.

Sitting on the opposite end of the bench to Thomas, she pulled a lime-green beanie hat over her cropped auburn hair – despite being spring, it was chilly. She ate a homemade sandwich and, not wanting to stare at him, focussed on the grey-brick department store opposite. She then snuck a sideways glance, frowning at the thing around his neck. Moving closer, she saw it was a small, laminated Dulton bus timetable. What the hell? She reached out to take it off, but shrank back before touching him – his face looked as serene as a sage. She hesitated, then stood, murmuring, "Bye Thomas."

When she told Noel about the bus timetable, he fiddled with papers on his desk. "The lad's body is sometimes used by the council or by businesses."

"Really? For what?"

Noel avoided her eye while polishing his glasses. "This and that. He... he doesn't seem to mind."

Was that true? She turned away, her forehead furrowed.

Alone in her bedsit that evening, Rose stared at two postcards she'd bought in town of Miro paintings. The first held things she felt she lacked in her life: colour, vivacity, imagination. The second she'd got for the title: *Figures at Night Guided by the Phosphorescent Tracks of Snails.* If only she had a phosphorescent track to take her somewhere...

Sleeping Thomas came to mind. On her laptop she found a recent article about him – actual name Thomas P. Mockchild – in the *Dulton Gazette*. It said that he was twenty and had developed the sleeping condition after being expelled from a local college where he'd studied art. There was no mention of his body's use by the council or businesses, but there was a photo taken at night of him sitting asleep, dressed up in a Father Christmas outfit, the High Street Christmas lights behind him like a glittery web. Rose shook her head; this seemed in questionable taste. From what she'd seen, he didn't seem a dressing-up-as-Santa type, more a grunge Buddha.

When awake, the article continued, Thomas was an unemployed supermarket shelf-stacker. His 'waking interests' were listed as chocolate, *The Simpsons,* and public painting. What did public painting mean? Rose didn't have a clue.

Two weeks later, trudging through a concrete shopping precinct on her way to work, she noticed a small crowd, and stopped to see what was going on. Dressed in a grey sweatshirt splattered with red flecks, Thomas was up a step-ladder, holding a can and painting a billboard. She watched him cover the entire advert for Corporation Cars in the colour of poppies. Imagining an expanse of the flowers there in the humdrum centre of town, her heart seemed to freeze, then pound. This was so unexpected. This was art surely!

A bald man beside her caught her eye and muttered, 'The lout's done this before, you know – vandalised ads with red or yellow paint."

Disliking Thomas described in that way, Rose edged her way to the front and called up to him, asking why he'd painted the billboard.

Thomas looked down from the ladder. "You get to see big bits of blue in the sky and green in the fields. You don't often get to see big bits of red." He had a soft, resonant voice.

"That's true," she said.

"Get a proper job, skiver," barked one voice.

"Stop vandalising billboards," cried another.

Rose felt sorry for Thomas as he slunk down the ladder and walked away. He had a gawky way of moving, as if avoiding imaginary potholes.

After stopping to buy coffee, Rose arrived at the library to find Thomas asleep on the bench. Was he alright? Did anyone care about him?

Inside, Rose told Noel about the billboard.

"Not again," Noel said. "Thomas has a history of painting all sorts of things in Dulton."

"Yes? What else?"

Noel said that one time, Low Street residents woke and opened their curtains to see only darkness filled with twinkling stars. It transpired that Thomas had quietly painted all the windows black during the night, but had left tiny holes through which the sun came, which created the illusion of stars.

"Wow! He turned day into night," said Rose.

"It cost the council five thousand pounds to clean up the mess." Noel told her that another time Thomas had painted the rocky outcrop on top of the hill north of the town: "Sky blue with the odd white cloud, so even on grey days the view that way looked clear and sunny."

The back of her neck tingled. "I really want to see that."

"I'm afraid the public and council considered it an eyesore, not in keeping with the nature of the place. Contractors took a week to scrub off the paint."

"Really?" Why did Dulton disapprove of Thomas's painting? Hearing about it was thrilling, like finding a phosphorescent trail.

From then on, Rose arrived at work each morning hoping Thomas would be on the bench. She hadn't made any friends in Dulton, and the place had an unreal feel, like it – and maybe she – existed only in black and white. Each evening she'd sit in her bedsit, doodling trees or flowers with a charcoal pencil. She'd check her texts – one from her mum or an old school friend – and then stare out at the moon, a cold, white stone in a sea of darkness. Whenever Thomas was on the bench, colour seeped back in. She'd remove whatever had been left on him – a *No Billposting in High Street* sign, an advertisement for a *Take That* tribute band – and eat lunch with his snoring self. She'd notice the crimson geraniums in the tubs on High Street, the turquoise diamonds on a passing woman's dress. Sometimes, even though Thomas was sleeping, she'd chatter away to him about the library: how Mr Pooks, the pub owner, took out *Mills & Boons*, while Miss Jay, who everyone thought simple, checked out Franz Kafka and Jorge Luis Borges.

One evening, flicking through a Sunday supplement magazine, Rose came across acclaimed 1950s paintings. She stared. Weren't they similar to Thomas's billboards? The next day she took photos of two painted billboards which hadn't (yet) been recovered by adverts and emailed them on spec to private galleries in London and Bristol, with a letter about 'local celebrity' (she exaggerated) Sleeping Thomas. Rose expected nothing to come of it – a shot in the dark. But a trendy man with a pea-green jacket and spiky blonde hair soon appeared in town; he was seen taking notes near a billboard. He came to find Rose at the library, introducing himself as Hugo Slemon from The Zarsttii Gallery in Bristol. She sucked in a breath and then smiled up at him.

"Do you know where I can find the artist?" he asked.

"He's outside right now, sleeping on the bench."

"The scruffy teenager with the ginger hair?"

"He's not a teenager."

75

"He's not what I was expecting."

Over coffee at Salman's Bistro, Hugo Slemon spoke excitedly about Thomas's billboards. "They're intriguing works of art. I can probably sell a few, too."

"I knew it." Rose tucked into her chocolate cake. "This town hates what he does, though." She told him about Thomas's art being erased by the council.

"I can understand Dulton Council finding it challenging, but as far as contemporary art goes, the town seems to have little imagination or taste. You, Rose, are thankfully an exception to that."

The words made her cheeks blush, her heart flush with warmth.

Hugo Slemon told her he'd negotiate with the council and take Thomas's billboards to exhibit. Rose was thrilled.

Two days later, men in white coats and gloves appeared in town, wrapping the billboards in cellophane, then putting them in a van. Word spread fast that Thomas's billboards were being taken away — some said by men in white coats, others said by an art gallery. Rose dashed out to see, silently cheering, but sadly Thomas was oblivious, deep as he was in a slumber.

A week later, when he finally awoke, Rose happened to be beside him. He yawned and stretched his arms. "Hi Thomas," she said, handing him a bottle of water.

He took a long swig and gave the bottle back. "Thanks. Do... I know you?" His narrow blue eyes took her in with a quiet curiosity.

Her cheeks reddened. "I'm Rose." She opened her bag and took out a print-out of an email catalogue she'd received from the Zarsttii Gallery. "Look at this!"

Frowning, he started to stand up.

"I'm not a weirdo, Thomas. Your billboards have been recognised as modern art."

On noticing the pictures of his billboards, he put a hand over his mouth. Underneath them was printed:

Red Billboard and Yellow Billboard
Thomas P. Mockchild
5m x 3 m
Industrial paint on advertising billboard
Price: (estimated) £4500 each

Ridges appeared across Thomas's forehead. Rose explained his art was being put on sale at a Bristol art gallery.

"You're taking the piss."

"No. This all happened while you were asleep." Rose read out:

"Thomas P. Mockchild, an untrained artist from Dulton (who suffers a mysterious, unique sleeping complaint), paints large-scale, monochromatic works, particularly in primary colours like red and yellow, which echo the emotionally intense, expanded colour-field works of Mark Rothko. But Mockchild's works offer a pop art or post-modern reworking of Rothko's paintings. They are executed not with oil on canvas, but with industrial paint on advertising billboards, thus offering not a statement of vibrant aesthetic <u>presence</u>, but an ironic comment on <u>absence</u> within modern consumer culture, as well as a radical erasure — through the act of painting itself — of this consumer culture."

Thomas gestured at the print-out. "This is for real?"

"Yes. I promise."

He grinned. "Oh, my god. This calls for chocolate and beer. Come to the pub to celebrate, Rose?"

She blushed. "I'd love to, but I have to be back at work." She gave him the print-out. "You must contact the gallery, okay?"

The next day Rose looked up from her desk at work to see a clean-shaven, handsome Thomas who smelled of aftershave. His auburn hair was tied back neatly in a pony-tail and his blue eyes gleamed. "You told that Bristol place about me," he said.

Warmth flushing through her, she nodded several times.

"Thanks. I can't believe it." He contemplated the books on the desk as if they were exotic food he'd never had a chance to try. "Some mates are coming round mine for a few drinks tonight to celebrate. Like to come?"

"Yes," she said. "Yes, please."

As Thomas wrote his address on an old bus ticket, Rose noticed he had a tattoo of an emerald dragonfly on his left hand, one of a turquoise hummingbird on his right. *How cool*, she thought. He gave the ticket to Rose and left. She fingered it, then slipped it into her pocket.

That evening, Rose arrived at the bedsit in a front-buttoning, lime-green (*eBay*) dress and thick black eyeliner and with butterflies in her stomach. The bedsit walls were painted azure blue, the ceiling and window-frames bold yellow. "What a funky place," she said.

"You look nice," said Thomas quietly.

Dressed in black jeans and a blue tee-shirt with *Pound-Shop Picasso* on it, he introduced her to the three lads with beers sitting on the floor. Smiling nervously, she sat on the sofa next to Thomas, and tucked her sweaty palms under her knees. But after Rose's glass had been filled a few times, she began to relax. Thomas's friends told anecdotes about *Lidl*, where they worked, and laughed raucously. Rose found herself chuckling, too. Thomas himself didn't say much. Was he contained or just shy? He often stared with curiosity into the distance, as if at something he wasn't sure existed. Once she caught him studying her, but his gaze flitted away as soon as she returned it.

She was drunk when his friends left at midnight singing "Thomas is the Champion" to the tune of the Queen song. Thomas rolled his eyes and grinned.

"Can I ask you something personal?" she said when they were alone.

"Go ahead."

"Don't you hate the way Dulton treats you? Leaves those signs on you?"

"Guess I'm used to it," he said with resignation.

"No one should be treated like that."

His gaze slid away. "Maybe I cope with stuff by pretending it's not happening."

"Is that why you sleep in public – you literally close down?"

He contemplated his lap. "Dunno. Who knows."

She rubbed her legs with her fingers. "I love your billboards. How did you even think of painting them?"

He smiled at the question. "Since a kid, I've had a need to paint. Not little things like paper, big things like houses, billboards, rocks. I love colour. It's kinda like life – or life at its best. Make sense?"

"Yes," she said. "Yes, it does."

"When I was nine, I painted a yellow sun on the front of our council house. Mum and Dad were always unhappy, always fighting. I thought they needed more sun... Dad did his nut, though, and shouted that I was a freak."

"You're eccentric, imaginative."

He turned his head away. "I'm a bloody freak."

"What about me? I've got a job, but it's not what I really want to do. I've got no friends in Dulton. Never had many friends." She let out a breath. "Who wants a podgy loser for a friend?" The bitchy Debbie Cleaver used to say that at school and the words still stung.

"You're lovely. I'd be proud to have you as my friend."

His words made her grin. "Sweet of you."

"What do you *really* wanna do?" he asked.

She'd wanted to go to art college after school, but her parents, ever cautious – they called it 'realistic' – had talked her into doing a vocational librarian course. "Something arty. I'm good at art. Got an 'A' for A-level."

"How cool." He stood up, struggling to balance, and fell over. They both laughed. "Sorry, I'm really pissed. Need to lie down," he said, and lay on the bed.

"I'm pissed too. Can... I lie next to you?"

"Sure."

Rose laid beside him, ensuring her body didn't touch his. She noticed his long, fine fingers – an artist's hands.

He twisted his head to look at her. "I'd like to paint something for you, Rose. What'd you like? Anything."

An idea came to her and she giggled. "On a clear blue day, paint some clouds pale pink, so the sky looks like it's full of marshmallows."

"Don't be daft."

"Um… how about painting something lime-green, my favourite colour."

"I'll see what I can do." He reached over and ran a tender finger down her cheek, then moved his lips gently towards hers.

Heat rose through her spine, but spotting a red wine smudge on his upper lip, she turned her head away. She'd only ever had one boy-friend, and while attracted to Thomas, drunken fumbles weren't her thing. "Sorry. I mean… we're too pissed… to know… you know… what we're doing."

But there was a familiar noise: snoring.

"Thomas?"

He snored on.

"Wake up."

More snores.

She got up to go home, but the room span and she collapsed back on the bed. Soon she was fast asleep too.

Rose woke in a hung-over daze and fully clothed. It took a minute to work out where she was. *Oh, god.* And what was the time? She had to get to work. She got up fast, and in the tiny kitchenette, downed a glass of water; her stomach heaved.

Thomas was sleeping as deeply as a sedated cat. "I should be off," she said, hoping he'd wake, but he didn't stir. As the place was a mess, with dirty glasses and empty bottles everywhere, she piled the glasses in the sink, managing to break one. *Shit!* Then she hurried home to shower.

At lunchtime, Rose's heart thrummed on seeing Thomas on the bench, but it sank when she realised he was in a slumber. A sign had been placed on his lap: *Bertie's Barber: BOGOF Haircuts.* Rose grabbed it and chucked it in a bin. Why did Dulton do this to him? And how long before he woke up again?

While Thomas slept on for twelve days through sun, rain, and Saturday shoppers, his billboards were displayed at the Zarsttii Gallery. Hugo Slemon emailed to tell Rose that he'd sold one quickly, and while she should have been thrilled, unease settled over her like a mist.

Rose's unease grew intense the night a fierce gale blasted the town. Lightning threw white bolts across the sky, the thunder sounded like a hollering army. Rose checked on Thomas twice during the night, wrapping an anorak around him the first time, putting a scarf on him the second. A hundred-mile-an-hour wind whipped through the town, tearing off roof tiles, and sweeping a lamb off its feet in the fields, then depositing it on High Street.

Next morning, Thomas was gone from the bench. Rose held her breath. Was he okay?

Shortly before the library closed, Noel spoke to Rose in a subdued tone, saying she should go to the recycling bins in Tesco car park. "Thomas is there."

"Was he blown there by the storm?"

"A customer just told me that some youths carried him."

She ran the quarter mile to Tesco, her heart hammering. She stopped by the recycling bins, panting for breath. A handful of people were gathered and two of them were laughing at Thomas who was asleep on a rickety old chair. On the ground by his feet were bottles, cardboard and a cracked television set; on his lap, a hand-written sign – *Rubbish 'Artist'*.

Rose grabbed the sign and flung it away. How dare people treat Thomas like this! "He's not just an artist, he's a human being. Remember that."

Thomas stirred for a moment, but didn't wake.

Rose called a taxi. The driver helped her get a sleeping Thomas into it and back to the library bench.

She sat guarding Thomas, turning over in her fingers a stone she'd found in her pocket. Noel turned up at 7pm to see if all was okay now. "Dulton shouldn't do these things to him," said Rose. "Someone needs to stop it."

Thomas sighed, but then snored on.

"I had a word with the police a few years ago," said Noel. "They weren't interested."

"You did?" She'd assumed Noel disapproved of Thomas.

"When he first started sleeping in public, I talked to various people. No one seemed to care. Eventually, I'm ashamed to say, I told myself it was all okay, even the signs put on him. But it wasn't. You've taught me that, Rose."

"Speak to the police again. I'll write to *Dulton Gazette*."

"Okay."

The next morning, when Thomas was gone once more from the bench, Rose's gut tensed. Where had they taken him this time?

"Try not to worry too much," said Noel. "He may have just woken up."

Late afternoon, when two customers told Rose that they'd seen Thomas ambling through town, relief flushed through her. After work, she hurried to his bedsit, but no one was there. She left a Miro postcard for him on which she'd written her mobile number. Back at her bedsit, she checked her texts every twenty minutes, but nothing came. She stared out of the window at the stars, little scars in the body of the night. At 10.30pm she gave up waiting and went to bed.

For the next few days, Rose sat on the bench each lunch-time, looking right, then left. Was he okay? Why hadn't he texted her?

She emailed the *Dulton Gazette*, complaining about how Thomas was treated; she asked them to do an article about his art, too. An editorial assistant replied saying they wouldn't be publishing the letter: Thomas himself had never complained and surely there was little harm in the young man being useful in some way? As for his 'art' – the editorial assistant said it was generally agreed to be in poor taste, an anti-social eyesore which the tax-payer paid the bill for cleaning up. Rose emailed back: *The Zarsttii Gallery clearly knows more about art than you. And as for 'poor taste', treating a vulnerable, talented young man the way Dulton does Thomas is the epitome of this.*

A senior editor later emailed Rose, apologising for the editorial assistant's 'unofficial views' and reassuring her that they would print her letter, but saying no to an article on Thomas's art as it 'didn't correspond with the Gazette's publishing priorities.' Rose sighed.

Noel told her he'd spoken to the police. "They're struggling with funding cuts and have no time for minor problems."

"Thomas's dignity isn't minor," said Rose.

She emailed Hugo Slemon to see if he'd heard from Thomas. He had apparently – Thomas was intending (if awake) to go to Bristol that Saturday to see his billboards in situ. In the meantime, he was planning a new artwork. Rose felt a spasm of irritation. Why hadn't Thomas invited her to Bristol? What new artwork?

On the fourth evening, there was still no contact from Thomas. She downed a bottle of wine and tore up a print-out of his red billboard. "He can find someone else to help him, the ungrateful sod."

As she was setting out for work the next day, a text came: *Rose. Go to Red Lion Square when you can. Thomas. :)*

Her heart thrummed. She'd go – it wasn't much of a detour – though he could damn well wait a bit before she texted him back. In Crouch Street she stopped abruptly and burst out laughing – the post-box had been painted lime green. In Elm Street the post-box was lime green, too. "Thomas!"

In Red Lion Square a crowd was assembled near two billboards. She pushed through the people, towards the front, and caught snippets of conversations:

"The lad should get a proper job."

"The lad needs arresting."

One billboard was painted white with looping lime-green writing across it:

Hey Dulton,

Strange as it may seem to some of you, I'm a human being. Remember that!

If you treat me like rubbish again, more than post-boxes will end up painted...

Way to go, Thomas, Rose thought.

On the other billboard was a rose. A five-foot, lime-green rose in an azure sky filled with pink fluffy clouds. The rose was painted with such naturalism, such loving precision, that Rose felt she could touch it.

The Cost of Starfish

Mersea Island, Essex, May 2055

Four lemons in a string bag lie next to a strand of seaweed on the potholed promenade. Dag scoops them up, puts them in his canvas bag. This is a good place to forage, close to the route by which goods are smuggled from ships anchored at sea, taken on little boats past Mersea Island and up to Colchester. It is a good day for it too, the sky cloudless, the sun warm. His gaze sweeps along the line where the waves greet the shore. He knows every bit of this coastline, as he knows every road, wood and field on the island. *Home*, he thinks, his heart swelling a little with affection.

His eyes settle on a ramshackle, abandoned ice cream kiosk. He has a memory from long ago of his mum, belly swollen with his soon-to-be sister Meg, buying him ice cream there when he was five; they had come in a car from Colchester on a clear spring day and sat on the beach to eat. But that was a different era, the Time of Plenty, one of cars and ice cream and mums. *No use thinking about the past.*

To the right, close to the shoreline, Meg is crouched down over something. Dag heads left, in the opposite direction, moving steadily closer to the sea, scanning the ground. Halfway between the promenade and the sea, he stops, his eyes widening. Two orange starfish lie before him. Where have they come from? He hasn't seen any in years. He lifts one up gently and places it on his palm. It moves an arm, tickling him. He feels an urge to throw it back into the sea, but this is his best find for ages and might fetch enough money for – what? – several months' worth of flour and some treats; there are those who will pay a lot for rare creatures like these. He gets out a small metal tin from his bag, puts the two starfish carefully in on a little bed of seaweed, and returns the tin to the bag. *Sorry, little fellas.*

"Dag!" His sister's shout startles him. She is standing up now and he follows her pointing finger. Near the crumbling steps, a way down Victoria Promenade, are four men headed in their direction. Thick-set with shaved heads, they are. Not islanders.

"Run!" he cries. Holding tight to his bag and with Meg on his tail, he shoots up the beach, across the promenade, over the pot-holed road, and along the pavement on the other side. He glances back — the men haven't given chase, not yet anyway; they have moved to the section of beach where Dag and Meg were and are scanning it. Turning left, the siblings pelt past the long line of derelict houses; Dag's leg muscles pump, his heart hammers. Near the old oak at the end, they squeeze through a gap in the fence and hide behind the old shed in the garden of what was once Seaview House. A three-storey house with the glass in its windows missing and ivy pouring from the top floor down the wall, a waterfall of green.

Dag crouches and pants for breath. Meg squats beside him, her skinny, tanned arms clenched round her bare legs. Her blue tee-shirt has mud stains and her unbrushed, dark hair hangs round her shoulders.

"Colchester Trolls, right?" Meg whispers.

"Think so." Dag speaks in a hushed, breathless tone.

"You think a boat sank or dropped its load?"

"Don't know. Didn't see anything. Did you?"

She shakes her head.

"Shush now," says Dag. "Should be safe here."

Where had the boat with the Trolls landed? The only thing left of the road that once joined Mersea Island to the mainland are concrete protrusions that stick out of the water like stubby toes.

Dag slips his hand into his bag, checking that the tin with the starfish is okay. *Sorry to shake you, little fellas.* Given their rareness, are they what the Trolls are here looking for? Did they somehow fall off a boat?

Shouts in the distance. Dag tenses and Meg takes out a small knife from a belt pouch, the blade glinting in the sunlight. She is fierce, even at sixteen; five years older, he wishes he had half her courage. She can be rash too, though. He mouths, "No knives." She scowls and kicks out at a tuft of grass with the toe of her trainers, but puts the knife away.

The voices come a bit closer. He presses his index finger to his lips: *shush*. Meg nods — *I know, I know.* Taking a breath and exhaling slowly, Dag tries to settle his pounding heart. He puts two fingers to the flat pendant stone on his leather thong, on which the goddess is carved. *Gaia keep us safe.* A cloud of yellow butterflies flutters near a huge buddleia bush. *All things pass, even Trolls.* The voices become more distant and he lets out a relieved breath. This was a good hiding place.

"Gone down East Road, probably," Meg whispers. "Think we're safe?"

"Five more minutes just to be sure."

A blackbird bursts into song and Dag twists his head to watch it in the silver birch. He spends a few minutes listening to it, trying to distract himself from the anxiety still prickling him.

Remembering the starfish, he takes out the tin from his bag, opens it, lifts one up, and places it on his palm.

Meg's brow creases and she seems about to say something, then stops herself. She touches the animal gently, but it still shrinks from her. "Why do we hardly ever see them now?"

"Because some time ago," says Dag, "they realised what a crap place the earth is, with so many humans and so much rubbish in the sea. One day they escaped on a ladder made out of fish-bones, hopped on a passing cloud, then floated up and up. They're stars now, swimming right up there." He points. "You can see them in the dark."

"Oh, yeah?" Meg arches her eyebrows, then fixes him with a serious stare. "You think they came from a Troll boat?"

"Dunno. Maybe."

"But you do intend to put them back in the sea, right?"

He thinks of his hunger pangs in February, when everyone was limited to two small meals daily, and of how the community needs to build stocks for next winter. "Imagine how much we can get for them."

"But they're Gaia's creatures."

"Biff will surely know someone we can sell them to in Colchester, who will keep them alive."

"No guarantees."

That is true. Although he's heard of collectors with aquariums, there are many people, not least the Trolls, who would kill and dry animals like this and sell them on as curios or amulets to rich northerners. He doesn't want to argue about this, though; has to be pragmatic. "Let's go. We need to warn the others."

"But—"

"Come on."

They make their way to Chapman Copse where they duck to avoid branches snagging their hair, and then drop onto the deserted Hills Road. Twenty minutes brisk walk brings them to a painted sign by the road, blue letters on a white background: *Welcome to The Children of Gaia Community.* On the bottom, someone has scribbled in looping longhand: *Love with all your butt — it's bigger than your heart.*

Dag glances back to check again that the Trolls haven't somehow managed to follow them. Over a mile in the distance, cresting the slight hill, are four figures walking in their direction. *Oh, hell, no!*

At Temple Barn, Dag sticks his head round the door — no one there. He bows quickly to the towering, green and silver Gaia painted on the end wall. He and Meg then hurry across Green Man Square, an expanse of grass where a bonfire is lit at night, and head towards the allotments fields. Most of the community are working in the fields. "Hey," Dag shouts, making beckoning gestures. "Come here!"

One by one, they hurry over.

Always speedy on his feet, Biff reaches Dag first. "What's up?"

"Four Colchester Trolls about a mile away. Saw them first down on the beach. They're now heading here."

"Christ almighty in me boots," says Biff. "Did a boat come a cropper?"

"Saw nothing. No idea what they want."

As people gather, word spreads that Trolls are on the island.

"Listen up!" Biff, who has a tall, wiry frame and shock of curly, dark hair, always commands attention. "Kids and Olds to Shepherd's Wood to hide. Stan, go with them. Now!"

The children and old folk do as they're told. Dag glances at Meg, but she stays put and stares defiantly. "I'm sixteen now," she says.

He has to admit she can handle herself as well as him these days and can run like the wind. "Okay, but any sign of trouble and you leg it."

"The rest of us will form a welcome party near Temple Barn," says Biff.

Middle-aged and always forthright, Amber steps forward. "Welcome? We should arm ourselves."

Amber gets disapproving looks. Here they believe in non-violence. "Gaia will protect us," says Biff.

"Against Trolls?" Amber lets out a dismissive sound, *tch*.

"Listen up," says Biff. "What are we to Trolls? Just weird folk on an island practically no one comes to anymore. Don't want to make ourselves 'something' by waiting with weapons. You get me?"

Amber frowns, then nods.

"Far more of us too." Biff instructs a few people to go and lock up the store sheds and barns, then tells the others to lock their caravans en route to Temple Barn. "Chop chop!"

Dag and Meg dash down South Path, past all the old caravans with their rusty hubcaps and paintings on the sides – rainbows, sunflowers. At their caravan, Dag throws the door open and jumps inside to the smell of damp and interior painted cobalt blue. Shelves of books, all filched from abandoned houses on the island, line one wall as well as quotes torn from old magazines – *Make Cakes not War, Reading is Sexy*. Dag and Meg ensure the windows are all firmly closed. He opens a cupboard to put his bag in.

"Keep the bag with you," says Meg. "The Trolls might have seen you with it. Just leave the starfish here."

"Good idea." There is little in it anyway, the foraging earlier hasn't yielded much.

Outside, Dag padlocks the caravan door. What if the Trolls were to set fire to their precious home? It doesn't bear thinking about.

Back at Temple Barn, nerves are raw, even though eighty or so of them against four is good odds, even when the four are Trolls. Dag hasn't met any Trolls close up since he and Meg ran away from Colchester eight years ago. He was thirteen and she only eight when they'd fled, a few months after their mum, like millions across the country, had died during the Great Floods. The Trolls had already got a reputation for violence by then, the gang warfare intensifying as the Time of Plenty collapsed and with it the old order. The siblings had been lucky to stumble across this remote place where attempts were being made to collaborate and anyone was welcome as long as they were prepared to work hard and accept the pagan ideas.

The islanders all fall silent as four stocky men with shorn heads round the bend. The ginger-bearded Troll at the front has one black eyepatch and wears a tee-shirt and jeans. He looks unarmed — if that word applies to someone with biceps the size of small footballs. The three Trolls behind him have large knife sheaths on their belts.

"It's Redbeard," mutters Meg beside him.

Dag begins to sweat. He recognises Redbeard as well as one other Troll, Slug, who has shoulders like a bull's. A memory flashes of Redbeard and Slug in Culver Square, Colchester, executing a man publicly, taking turns to stab him; they had told the large crowd of onlookers, which included Dag and Meg, that the man had betrayed them.

"Go to the back, and if there's any trouble, run for the wood," he says.

Meg shoots him a troubled look and then disappears into the crowd.

Dag slides a few steps further back himself, trying to settle his growing panic. *Breathe in, one, breathe out, two.* He can see the Trolls over Amber's shoulder.

The four Trolls halt in a line fifteen or so paces from the crowd. Tattoos festoon Redbeard's arms.

Biff steps forward and clears his throat. "Welcome. How can we help you?" The lack of wind means his words will be easily heard across the gap.

Slug snorts. "Forgotten how full of 'peace and love' crap you lot are."

Redbeard shoots Slug a brief look as if to say: *quiet!* "A boat sank last night," he tells Biff. "Had stuff in we want back. Seen anything unusual on the shore?"

"Tell us what to look for and we'll keep an eye out."

"Why would you do that?"

"Why wouldn't we?"

"Two of you down on the promenade earlier. Who was that?"

Biff turns, looking for Dag, and finding him in the crowd, beckons him with a hand. "This lad here and his younger sister."

As Dag forces himself to move forward to the very front, his heart thumps.

Redbeard's hands are fisted on his hips. "Seen any starfish on the beach? Might be a small reward in it for you."

Dag's throat feels dry. So the starfish *were* on the Troll boat originally. He reminds himself that the Trolls probably intend to kill and preserve them. "No. Only lemons, an apple."

"That the bag you had on the beach?"

"Yes."

Redbeard takes several steps forward alone, until a third of the way to the crowd, and holds out his palm. "Let's see."

Dag throws a searching look at Biff who nods for Dag to go ahead.

Palms sweating, Dag walks towards the Troll and stops a good yard away. *Thank Gaia I took out the starfish earlier.* He takes the bag off his shoulder and holds it out at arm's length. Redbeard accepts it and searches inside. As Dag instinctively starts to retreat, Redbeard says, "Stay there." Dag freezes.

Redbeard looks up from the bag, his dark eyes sharp like flint. "Not much in here. This all there was on the beach?"

"Y... yes."

Redbeard offers the bag. "Take it."

As Dag goes to do so, he is grabbed by a strong hand, spun round, and one of his arms wrenched up painfully behind his back. "Ouch." When a knife is put to his throat, his heart thuds so loud he can hear it in his ears. Where did the knife come from? He hadn't seen one on the man.

"I'm asking again. Seen any starfish?" growls Redbeard.

Icy fear grips Dag. Should he lie again or be honest? "I..."

"He's an honest lad." Biff takes two steps forwards and holds up his palms in a gesture of appeal. "Please put the knife down. We'll help any way we can."

Meg bursts out of the crowd, halting beside Biff. "Please! I can help. I was down on the beach too. I know exactly where the starfish are, but my brother doesn't."

"Expect me to believe this little shit doesn't know?" says Redbeard.

The knife nicks Dag's skin and he winces. *Gaia protect me.*

"It's true," exclaims Meg. "My brother's a soft sod and would have thrown those critters back in the sea. I'm made of stronger stuff. I saw them and picked them up when he wasn't looking and hid them in a tin. I knew they could be sold on."

She sounds convincing even if she is lying, but will Redbeard believe her?

"Get them now," Redbeard says.

"It'll take a few minutes." She gestures to the crowd behind Biff. "You hurt my brother and you'll answer to all of us, right?" She dashes off.

Dag can smell Redbeard's pungent body odour close behind and tries not to glance down at the blade still against his throat. Meg was shrewd to remind the Trolls of just how many people are on Dag's side, several of whom, including Amber, now move forward to buttress Biff. Dag's gaze darts anxiously over the crowd. Would Redbeard risk killing him with these odds? *Gaia protect me. Oh, please protect me.*

Meg, out of breath, soon reappears with the tin. Biff mutters something to her and she begins to walk slowly towards Redbeard, holding it out.

"Slug. You check they're all there." Redbeard calls to his fellow Troll.

For Christ sake, don't make my mistake of going too near him, thinks Dag. He wants to blurt that out loud; the knife at his neck gags him. Thankfully, Meg, who has a good head on her, sets the box down on the grass halfway to Slug and then retreats. "They're in there." She points.

Slug strides forward, grabs it, and opens it. "Only two here." He walks the box towards Redbeard.

"That's all I found, I promise." The pitch of Meg's voice goes up. "How many were there then?"

"Three," says Redbeard.

Fear slips down Dag's spine and he has to make a conscious effort not to tremble.

"The tides being what they are, that third starfish could be anywhere between here and Brightlingsea – that's miles and miles of shoreline and sea." Biff glances at the fellow community members beside him, then looks back at Redbeard. "You've got two-thirds of the starfish back. Now put the knife down."

Slug mutters, "Let's go," but quietly so only Redbeard and Dag can hear.

As Redbeard releases Dag, he shoves him away hard. Dag tumbles backwards, landing with a thud on his bottom.

Redbeard points the knife at Dag. "You're lucky I didn't slit your throat."

Dag flinches; instinctively his hands go up to shield his face.

But Redbeard turns his attention to the crowd. "You lot come across the other starfish and I want it. I mean that. Try to sell it on to someone else in Colchester? I'll hear about it and come back with more men to burn down your barns."

Dag knows that's not an empty threat: the Trolls set fire to storage barns full of grain in Abberton last year.

Redbeard snatches the tin off Slug and, ordering the other Trolls to follow, swings around and strides off. A minute or so later, when the Trolls vanish round the bend, fear starts to uncurl from Dag's heart and he jumps up. *Thank Gaia.* He hurries over to the others. A thought presses into his head, something familiar yet half-forgotten but which he can't articulate completely.

"Thank Gaia for keeping you safe," says Biff.

"Meg played a part too." Dag feels a flush of gratitude for his quick-thinking, bold sister. Then he recalls the starfish. No way will they be safe now. "But the starfish…"

"Meg did what was best." Biff pats Dag on the shoulder. "You're okay, Dag. That's the main thing."

Meg stares. "Your neck!"

He presses two fingers lightly to it and, when he then looks at them, there is a little blood. His blood. He feels light-headed, makes an effort to steady himself.

Meg throws her arms round him. "You alright, bruv?"

"Yes," he says, hoping he sounds reassuring.

But sadness unexpectedly pushes into his throat like an undertow sending a boat off course. He clenches his eyes shut so no one can see his tears and embraces Meg. What he could only half-grasp just now strikes him fully, something he first learned during the collapse of the Time of

Plenty: *any life or way of life, even if seemingly solid and stable, can be ruptured in the blink of an eye.* He hugs Meg some more.

She lets go of him and steps back. "I've got a confession. I did find the other starfish on the beach, but tossed it straight back into the sea before you saw it. I couldn't admit that to the Troll or he'd have known I was lying earlier."

Biff strokes her head affectionately. "I guessed *you* were actually the one keen to chuck them back."

And Dag's heart lifts and strengthens as an image comes of the starfish alive and free under the waves.

Ticket to Nowhere

"Destination?" asked the woman in the railway ticket office. She had pink blotchy skin and dark bags under her eyes.

"Nowhere," I said.

"Single or return?"

"Can I get an open return for the next train?"

"Not during peak hours."

I sighed. "Okay, single then." I had no idea how long I would be in Nowhere, but had taken a few days off work, anyway.

"That'll be £35."

"For a one-way ticket to Nowhere? That's a complete rip-off!"

"Take it or leave it," the woman said flatly. "Nowhere's the cheapest destination on offer. I can do Elsewhere for £44 or Somewhere for £52. We have a special offer to Everywhere for £99, which includes free vouchers for a Nirvana milk-shake and Armageddon hamburger."

"I need a ticket to Nowhere." I opened my purse and handed over the money. "When does the next train leave?"

"In five minutes from platform three."

I took the ticket, picked up my suitcase, and followed the signs to platform three. Pacing resolutely, I was conscious of the click-click of my high heeled boots on the floor. It was dark outside apart from the dim lamps that lit the platform at intervals. A lonely half-moon was hovering high above, and I turned up the collar of my woollen overcoat against the chill of the night.

A train slid out of a tunnel, then steadied to a halt. I found a seat in a carriage with few passengers. The train chugged off without enthusiasm into the night, and peering out of the window, I could see nothing, only darkness ahead, darkness behind. I felt anxious to be heading to Nowhere, but I had to go there. I'd much have rather been at home, curled up on the sofa with a novel.

My mind flitted once more to the last encounter with Marcus seven months ago: him begging me for one more chance, me striding out angrily with a: "You promised me you'd quit the drugs, so go to hell." I thought too of the message I'd got two days ago from a mutual acquaintance, saying he'd heard Marcus was in a 'dangerously bad way' and was desperate to speak to or see me. The chap hadn't got Marcus's address or phone number, but knew he was in Nowhere. The message, which still sent a sliver of fear down my spine, was the reason I was on this train.

My rumination was interrupted by the train stopping at a station. An elegant, blonde woman got on, in her forties probably and with a crimson velvet overcoat and matching lipstick. She sat opposite me, her back straight as a pen, and smiled courteously, then she took out a paperback and began to read. I surreptitiously clocked the title – *The Dark Descent of Elizabeth Frankenstein* – but hadn't heard of it. I settled down with my own novel to pass the time.

A while later she put her book down and caught my eye. "You're heading to Nowhere?" she asked.

"Yes." I placed my book on the table.

She regarded me confidently. "You don't look the sort."

"Pardon?"

"The sort who goes to Nowhere."

"Don't a lot of people go there at sometime?"

Her wide-set, intelligent eyes took me in. "Right now you look to me like the kind who'd be headed Somewhere."

Was that assumption based on my appearance? "How do you know? Sorry, but you don't know me."

"How can I put this? You know those clocks which give off a faint glow at night? People such as you are like that. People from Nowhere aren't glowers; they absorb light, not give it off."

I was unsure about the allusion to glowing; it made me sound radioactive.

"People from Nowhere seem so grey," she continued.

"And I'm wearing a cerise top?"

"I mean the people from Nowhere look like they've been defeated by life. By a significant score: Life-8, People-0."

There was something I liked about the woman, her directness perhaps. "You're right I don't live in Nowhere," I said. "I'm just trying to find someone there. What about you?"

She let out a weary breath. "My poor old aunt's lived in Nowhere for four years. I visit her occasionally, though have to admit I dread it. Who are you looking for, if you don't mind me asking?"

I hesitated, but I was warming to her or to company on this journey at least. "My ex, Marcus. We split up seven months ago, on my 26th birthday actually."

"I'm sorry."

"Don't be." Although a sensitive, creative man who used to pen me love poems illustrated with his cartoon drawings, Marcus was messed up, too. "We were close, but he got into things that weren't good for him and I wasn't happy about it. After we split, he got more heavily into the things that weren't good for him, lost his job, got into debt, and I gather ended up Nowhere, poor bloke."

Wrinkles spread over her forehead. "You're here to try and rescue him?"

"Yes... No... Maybe." What was my motivation? I'd dated a couple of other men briefly since, neither of whom had replaced Marcus in my affections, but I didn't really want to rekindle things, especially if he was in Nowhere and even though I knew his addictions were the consequence of a tough childhood. "An acquaintance told me Marcus was in a bad way and was asking to see me." I glanced down and rubbed my hands on my brown cord skirt. "I feel a bit guilty about what happened, you see. We were in love when I left him."

A look of concern came over her face. "You know you're probably onto a losing battle. It's hard for a person to get out once they're stuck in Nowhere."

"Well, maybe I can offer a helping hand."

"You need a crane not a hand to lift someone out of Nowhere."

My heart dipped. "You think?"

"A word of warning: don't spend too long in the place. It's like sinking sand, sucks you under."

"Cheers." I shifted in my seat, unnerved.

The woman returned to her paperback and we sat in silence. My mood became darker, like it was being infiltrated by shadows. I turned to stare at the window, but saw only my own dim reflection – at night, train windows become like ghostly mirrors. Finally, we arrived at Nowhere Station. I got off, saying goodbye to the woman.

Coming out of the station, I had my first glimpse of Nowhere: shops protected by anxious metal grates, boarded-up houses glazed with graffiti, gutters swollen with kebab wrappers, tatty billboards promising imbecilic illusions of happiness. I walked nervously down Station Road, past Hades' Hamburgers, Kali's Kebabs, Cheap Skates, Desolate Designs, Budget Drugs, and The Oblivion Inn. In an odd way, Nowhere could be anywhere.

I bought a takeaway pizza and was relieved to find the Despond Hotel two streets further down, where I'd booked a room. The faded-orange bedcover and cracked window overlooking a dirty alleyway told me why the price was so cheap. I ate the pizza listening to police sirens in the distance. Before getting undressed, I took out one of Marcus's cartoons I still kept in my purse – a sunflower on which was my face, a bumble bee wearing his face, and the words: *love is as lovely as it can be, you are the nectar and I am the bee.* Holding it in my fingers, I felt a surge of sadness. Then I folded it away quickly and went to bed.

My dreams brought no solace. They were full of Marcus being sucked down a gutter, his naked body covered in graffiti.

I didn't have anything to go on so for the next couple of days I searched high and low on foot. I kept an eye out as I passed homeless people, half expecting to discover him in some doorway. As Marcus liked the outdoors, I spent time in Pluto Park, wandering across its field of emaciated turf. In the notorious Bleeding Keel Pub I was hit at by some drunk for no reason. Twice. I rushed out of the place, my heart pounding.

In Doldrums Drive, a middle-aged man was sitting in a burnt-out car, twiddling the dials on a defunct radio and humming along to its non-existent tunes. Nearby, a teenage boy sat in a boat in a waterless pond, staring out at something I couldn't see. In Inertia Road, a ginger-haired girl was asleep in a wheelbarrow, covered by a blanket of tabloid newspaper. Further down an abandoned crane had *Fuck-All Works* painted on it in red.

Where the hell was Marcus? Was he okay? As my search continued, so my spirits became flatter, as if being steamrollered by a gloomy tank. Late on the second day, I sat on a broken-down milk-float along Magdalene Road. I lowered my head and let out a long breath; it felt like the whole stinking heart of Nowhere was seeping into my soul.

A short, white-haired man with a newspaper, sitting hunched on the other end of the milk-float, twisted his head to me. His kindly face had liver spots on the cheeks. "Death is the invincible enemy of man," he said.

I frowned. "I beg your pardon?"

"I said, 'Death is the invincible enemy of man'."

"I know, but it's a pretty odd thing to say to a stranger."

"Sorry." He shrugged. "Just a phrase from my paper. A bit pompous perhaps, but it's written on the obituaries page whenever another youngster is found dead."

"I'm sorry someone's died."

"Don't be. Dying's fashionable around here. All the young blokes are doing it."

A shadow flitted across my mind. "What was the name of the chap who died?"

He peered at the newspaper. "Um... Marcus Kingsfleet."

Heart thudding, I stood up, approached him, and put out my hand. "Please let me see?"

He handed me the paper, open at the obituaries page. There was a tiny photo of Marcus with his sharp cheekbones and cropped black hair. I lowered the paper and burst into tears.

"I'm guessing this isn't your normal response to the obituaries page," he said.

I glared at him through my tears.

"Sorry if that came across as flippant. It's just death is a way of life here. I assume you knew the poor bloke then?"

"Yes." *Oh god.* Marcus dead. I handed the paper back and wiped my tears with the back of my hand. But my grief segued quickly to a hollow, empty feeling, like I wanted to lie down and give up, like life had done a runner on a train leaving me stranded at the station. Maybe that was what Nowhere did to you. Maybe this was how Marcus had felt too?

The man cleared his throat. "None of my business really, but you don't look like you're from round here. You look a nice girl, maybe from Somewhere. Bit of advice from an old-timer: this place drags you in, feeds off you from the bones outwards. Get the hell out of Nowhere before Nowhere gets the hell into you."

His brown eyes seemed hollow as wells, yet his words were full of wisdom. I knew I couldn't help Marcus now, but needed to help myself. "Thanks," I murmured.

I forced myself to walk back towards the hotel, even though it felt like moving through solid air. At the hotel, I made myself pack my belongings and then phoned for a taxi, which took me to Nowhere Station.

"Destination?" asked the woman at the ticket office.

"Anywhere Else."

"Single or return?"

"Single please."

Acknowledgements

'Snapshots of the Apocalypse' won the Tate Modern short story competition TH2058, 2009.

'Haunted by Paradise' was first published as 'Eva's Eden' in *On the Day of the Dead*, Blackpear Press (2016), pp.46-51.

'The Wings of Digging' was published in a much shorter version in *Writers' Forum*, February 2020, #220, pp.39-43

'The Job Lottery' was first published as 'All for Ella' in *The Magic Oxygen Literary Prize 2018* (2018), MOLP Press, pp.98-105.

'Knitting to Oblivion' was first published in *Aestes 2016*, Fabula Press, p.147-160.

'The Colour of Dulton' was first published in *Tasting Notes* (2018), Ouen Press.

'Ticket to Nowhere' was first published online in *Serendipity*, #6, 2010 http://www.magicalrealism.co.uk/issue.php?issue=6

End Note

I'd like to thank all those who gave feedback on these stories, particularly Dot Schwartz, Petra McQueen and Ruth Arnold, and also Joe Gillett, Sue Allen, Joss Morton, Richard Dunn, and Richard Cooper. Thanks also to Anne Hamilton for her excellent editing. And I'm so grateful to Isabelle Kenyon for accepting this book for publication and for all her enthusiasm and enterprise at Fly on the Wall Press.

I'd like to express my appreciation to those who have offered support through a tough health time, particularly the very kind and practical Ann 'Dids' Wimhurst and my dear and playful friend Ruth 'Twiglet' Arnold. Thanks also to Charlie 'Kafka Boots' Turner, Amy Smith, Sue 'Dog Aunty' Dickenson, Coryn 'Origami Octopus' Smethurst, Joss 'Rock Chick' Morton, Petra McQueen, Dot Schwarz, Poppy Palin, Dawn Cattermole, Nick Mockridge, Emma Ashby, Rachel 'Burchog' Burch, Sally Greenwood, Sue Allen, Chris 'Rainforest' Redston, Angelina and Dave Whittaker Cook, and Dave Slavinskas. Thanks also to the hugely competent Millie Millard.

Finally, I'd like to thank my dear Claire T-H for her surreal chats and, um, dazzling hairdresser abilities. And thanks to dogs, seahorses, trees, rivers and chocolate for existing.

Sixty percent of author royalties will be divided equally between two charities, Invest in M.E. and the M.E. Association. M.E. is a complex multi system disease which afflicts about 250,000 people in the U.K., a quarter of whom are housebound or bedbound. The illness, which has many disabling symptoms, has often been maligned and misrepresented as 'fatigue'. More information about M.E. is available at http://www.investinme.org and https://meassociation.org.uk

About the Author

Katy Wimhurst is a writer and visual poet. Her short fiction has appeared in numerous magazines and anthologies including *The Guardian, Shooterlit, Cafe Irreal, Ouen Press, Fabula Press, Magic Oxygen Literary Prize,* and *To Hull and Back.* Her visual poetry has been published in magazines such as *The Babel Tower Notice Board, 3am, Ric Journal, AngelHouse Press, Steel Incisors,* and *Talking All The Time About Strawberries.* She studied social anthropology (and Mexican Surrealism at postgraduate level) and has worked in teaching and publishing. She lives by a pretty river, adores trees, and suffers from the neuroimmune illness M.E.

About Fly on the Wall Press

A publisher with a conscience.
Publishing high quality anthologies on pressing issues,
chapbooks and poetry products, from exceptional poets around
the globe.
Founded in 2018 by founding editor, Isabelle Kenyon.

Other publications:

Please Hear What I'm Not Saying

Persona Non Grata

Bad Mommy / Stay Mommy by Elisabeth Horan

The Woman With An Owl Tattoo by Anne Walsh Donnelly

the sea refuses no river by Bethany Rivers

White Light White Peak by Simon Corble

Second Life by Karl Tearney

The Dogs of Humanity by Colin Dardis

Small Press Publishing: The Dos and Don'ts by Isabelle Kenyon

Alcoholic Betty by Elisabeth Horan

Awakening by Sam Love

Grenade Genie by Tom McColl

House of Weeds by Amy Kean and Jack Wallington

No Home In This World by Kevin Crowe

The Goddess of Macau by Graeme Hall

The Prettyboys of Gangster Town by Martin Grey

The Sound of the Earth Singing to Herself by Ricky Ray

Inherent by Lucia Orellana Damacela

Medusa Retold by Sarah Wallis

Pigskin by David Hartley

We Are All Somebody

Aftereffects by Jiye Lee

Someone Is Missing Me by Tina Tamsho-Thomas

Odd as F*ck by Anne Walsh Donnelly

Muscle and Mouth by Louise Finnigan

Modern Medicine by Lucy Hurst

These Mothers of Gods by Rachel Bower

Andy and the Octopuses by Isabelle Kenyon

Sin Is Due To Open In A Room Above Kitty's by Morag Anderson

Fauna by Dr. David Hartley

How To Bring Him Back by Claire HM

History of Forgetfulness by Shahe Mankerian

No One Has Any Intention Of Building A Wall by Ruth Brandt

The House with Two Letter-Boxes by Janet H Swinney

Social Media:

@fly_press (Twitter)

@flyonthewall_poetry (Instagram)

@flyonthewallpress (Facebook)

www.flyonthewallpress.co.uk